THE SECRE

Raven Hill Mysteries

THE SECRET
OF BANYAN BAY

Raven Hill Mysteries 8

Emily Rodda
&
John St Claire

Hodder
Children's
Books

a division of Hodder Headline plc

Series concept copyright © Emily Rodda 1994
Text copyright © Ashton Scholastic 1994

First published in Australia in 1994 by
Ashton Scholastic Pty Limited

First published in Great Britain in 1998
by Hodder Children's Books

A Catalogue record for this book is
available from the British Library

ISBN 0 340 71463 8

Printed and bound in Great Britain by
Clays Ltd, St Ives plc

Hodder Children's Books
A Division of Hodder Headline plc
338 Euston Road
London NW1 3BH

Contents

1

Welcome to paradise

'Welcome to paradise,' the driver said. He turned and grinned back at us. 'End of the line, kids. Everyone off.'

The Teen Power gang stumbled off the bus. All six of us—Elmo, Liz, Richelle, Sunny, Nick and me—breathed a deep breath of fresh air and stretched our legs. After a five-hour ride just being able to stand up was like paradise—but Nuk Nuk really was beautiful.

'Is this it?' Richelle asked. 'Are we here?'

'We're *here*,' I said, 'but we're not *there* yet.'

'Give it a rest, Tom,' she yawned. 'Where's your Dad's house?'

The main street of the town was clogged with summer tourists dodging the racks of shirts and beach towels that spilled out onto the footpaths. It was like one long outdoor shopping mall, but neat and tidy compared to Raven Hill.

'Look at that surf!' drooled Nick.

I looked over at the beach as a long wave curled, carrying a line of surfers towards the headland at the other end. One board went down and an unexpected chill shot through me.

The sea has always scared me. Other people seem to think of it as some blue, sparkling playground. But I've never seen it like that.

Maybe that's because I've never learned to swim properly. Or maybe it's *why* I've never learned. I can't remember a time when I wasn't scared of the sea. It's always seemed to me just a big watery graveyard filled with dead ships, and sharks and skeletons. And I've never been able to get the fear out of my head.

Of course it's something I keep to myself. I've got enough problems without people thinking I'm a wimp about water as well.

'Well?' Richelle said. 'Where are we?'

'This is Nuk Nuk,' I said. 'Dad's place is in Banyan Bay. You remember. I only told you a thousand times. We have to catch a local bus to get there.'

Elmo and Sunny groaned. Richelle pouted.

'Not another bus ride!' Nick complained, arching his back. 'That last one gave me permanent curvature of the spine. If I bent over and grabbed my ankles, you could roll me the rest of the way.'

'Settle down, children,' I said. 'It's simple. We wait for the bus right here. And it's only a forty-five minute trip this time. We're nearly there.'

'That's right,' Liz sighed happily. 'We're nearly there. And isn't it *great*? To be going to a peaceful, friendly place. To get away from the city. And the traffic. And rush. And noise.

And pollution. And crime. And cockroaches. And . . .'

Everyone agreed. And I had to admit, it was nice. Sea or no sea, I was glad to be out of town. Summer holidays at home in Raven Hill were a bore. It was good to get away. And, of course, my stepfather, Brian, is a teacher so he's at home all the time in the summer. Just getting away from Brian is a holiday in itself.

It wasn't going to be all holiday for us in Banyan Bay. Dad had work for us to do. He's an artist, and he'd built a studio extension on his new house. He wanted help painting it. That was why the whole gang had come with me. We've got this business called Teen Power Inc. We say in our ads: 'We'll do Anything.' So Dad hired us. But, knowing him, there'd be lots of time off so we could muck around too.

I hoped Dad's new place would be okay. That the gang would like it, I mean. I hadn't seen it myself yet, because Dad and his wife, Fay, had only moved to Banyan Bay a couple of months before.

I liked their old place but Dad said that the new place was better because it was right on the water.

'Nuk Nuk is nice nice,' said Nick, looking around. 'I could live in a place like this—for a while, anyway. Plenty of money to be made round here, wouldn't you say?'

Typical of Nick to see paradise as a money-making opportunity.

I walked across the street to the newsagency and was buying a sketchbook when the bus arrived. By the time I came out the gang was all on board and the driver was tooting the horn to tell me he was ready to leave.

The bus was a tatty old thing with 'Sheila' written on the side next to the driver's window.

'Your mates tried to get me to leave without you,' the driver joked, as I climbed in, stuffing my sketchbook into my shoulder bag and trying to pull my wallet out at the same time. 'But I didn't think that'd be the best idea.'

He slammed the bus into gear and, with a roar and a jerk, we were off.

'What are you lot after in Banyan?' he shouted, over the roaring of the engine.

'Peace and quiet!' I yelled back, holding tightly to a shuddering rail so I wouldn't fall flat on my face. I didn't mention Dad. The last thing I needed was to have to explain why he lived in Banyan Bay and I lived in town.

The driver laughed and changed gear. 'Well, you'll get plenty of that, son,' he shouted to me over the sound of Sheila's struggling engine. 'Nothing ever happens in Banyan.'

●

We rattled along the highway. It was hot even with all the windows open. Sunny and Elmo stretched out over empty seats with their hats covering their faces, pretending to sleep.

Richelle was reading—well, looking at the pictures in—a magazine called *Simply Stylish*. From what I could see over her shoulder everything in it was hideous and cost a fortune. I guess simple style isn't my thing.

For a while I wasn't awake or asleep. I don't know what I was. All I know is that every time the bus hit a bump the window I was leaning against bashed me on the skull.

Nick sat across the aisle, wide awake, as if he was thinking through one of his business schemes. In fact this time it wasn't anything to do with making money.

'Okay, you guys,' he said finally. 'There are these three guys and they want to play cricket.'

'Three guys? An Irishman, an Englishman and an American, I suppose,' Liz said.

Nick frowned. 'It's not a joke. It's a puzzle,' he said. 'Okay, these three guys only have one dollar each—three dollars all together. You listening, Elmo?'

Elmo shifted on his seat.

'Unfortunately,' he mumbled from under his hat.

'Okay, so they've lost their only cricket ball. So they go to buy one.'

Sunny got up and turned around in her seat.

'What kind of cricket ball can you get for three bucks?' she demanded.

'Sunny, that's not the point—' Nick began. Then he gave up. For Sunny Chan, even a puzzle has to be realistic.

'Okay, okay. It's a second-hand one, Sunny,' he drawled. 'These guys reckon they can buy a pretty good *used* cricket ball for three bucks.'

Sunny nodded. This was satisfactory. 'Keep going,' she said.

'Thank you. So they see this mate of theirs coming

5

along and one of them says, "Hey, Ben, do you know where we can buy a used cricket ball?" Ben knows where to get everything. "My cousin has one," he tells them. "Will he sell it for three dollars?" one of the guys asks. "I think so," Ben says.'

'Nick, will you get to the *point*,' Liz said. 'Where's the puzzle?'

'Wait for it. Okay, so Ben goes off with a fistful of change—three dollars, okay? He finds his cousin and he says, "Do you still have that cricket ball for sale?" His cousin shows him the ball and it's kind of daggy so Ben says, "I'll give you two-fifty for it."'

'Everybody wants to make a profit,' Elmo muttered.

'No, Ben just reckons it's not worth three bucks. Anyway, the cousin agrees to the two-fifty and Ben gives him the money and walks away with the cricket ball plus fifty cents.'

Richelle looked up from her magazine.

'What's this all about?' she asked. 'Could you start from the beginning again?'

'Forget it, Richelle,' Liz said quickly. 'I'll tell you later. Come on, Nick, get on with it.'

'Okay, now Ben has a problem: how is he going to split the fifty cents three ways? I mean, he can't give his friends sixteen and two-thirds cents each, can he?'

'Why doesn't he give them each ten cents back and keep the twenty cents for himself?' Sunny asked. 'Sort of as payment for his trouble.'

'You've heard this, haven't you?' Nick asked.

'No I haven't.'

'Well that's exactly what he does,' Nick said. 'He goes back to his mates and tells them he got the ball for two dollars seventy. He gives them the ball and gives them each ten cents back. They're happy. He's happy. He wasn't trying to make a profit on the deal, but it was easier to pocket the twenty cents than try to split it.'

'So what's the problem?' Liz asked.

'Here's the puzzle: they each paid ninety cents. Like they gave him a dollar each and he gave them each back ten cents, right?'

'Right,' Liz said.

'Three times ninety is two dollars seventy, right?'

'Right?'

'Two dollars seventy plus the twenty cents he still has in his pocket is two dollars ninety, right?'

'Right.'

'So what happened to the other ten cents?' Nick asked.

Everyone was quiet. Elmo took the hat off his face and sat up. I opened my eyes. Nick was looking very smug.

'Now wait a minute,' Elmo said. 'Run that by us again, will you?'

'Just think about it,' Nick said. 'But I'll bet you can't figure it out. How about you, Tom? You like puzzles.'

He was right, I do. But not when I'm half-asleep. I closed my eyes again and leaned against the window.

'Later,' I said. 'Much later.'

2

Banyan Bay

Nick was just finishing his cricket-ball puzzle for the third time when Sheila chugged into Banyan.

One look, and my heart sank.

Banyan Bay was no Nuk Nuk. Most of the shops on the little main street were boarded up, and there was no surf on the beach because of the long breakwater that hooked out into the sea in the distance.

The town wasn't awful or anything. It looked really peaceful, like Dad had said it was. But it was too peaceful, if you know what I mean. Not so much sleepy, as dead.

I looked around for Dad but didn't see him at first. Then a tall, skinny shape unfolded itself from a bench outside Skinner's General Store and started walking towards the bus.

It was him.

He was wearing very torn, very faded paint-stained jeans and a fringed leather sleeveless jacket with no shirt. The felt bushie's hat was so wide that I couldn't see his face. I was used to seeing his hair in a ponytail, but today it was plaited into two braids that hung down down to the middle of his deeply-tanned chest.

'Hey, look, the natives are restless,' drawled Nick. 'Love the plaits!' He obviously didn't dream that this vision was to be his host for the week.

I felt myself starting to blush. I realised that I hadn't been quite prepared for this. My friends' reactions to my drop-out father.

Liz glanced at me, quickly sized up the situation and rushed in to help. 'Hey, Tom, that's not your dad, is it?' she said loudly. 'Wow! You never told me he was a hippie.'

'Oops,' muttered Nick

Richelle sniggered.

Dad wandered up to the bus as we clambered out.

'Welcome,' he said. He hugged me, and grinned at the others.

'So you're Teen Power Inc.,' he said. 'Nice to meet you all at last. Well, I hope your power's well stoked up. You're going to need it. I'm going to work you to the bone.'

Richelle stared at him with wide-open, frightened blue eyes. I knew he was joking, but she didn't. I half-expected her to squeak, 'Oh, is that the time? Well, I must be off!' and jump straight back on the bus.

Fortunately, Dad noticed the look and laughed. 'Just kidding,' he said.

Richelle smiled nervously.

The bus driver had been watching all this with a broad grin on his face. He raised his hand to us. 'See ya,' he said.

He cranked Sheila into gear, revved the engine, and roared off.

I must admit I felt a bit lost as I watched him go. And the others were feeling the same if the looks on their faces were any guide. It was like the old bus was our only link with civilisation—and it was disappearing, leaving us stranded.

All of a sudden I was wondering what a week alone with Dad and Fay and the gang was going to be like. I don't know why I hadn't thought about it before. I just hadn't. But now I was making up for lost time.

Dad took us to where his ute was parked outside the general store, and helped us put our bags into the back.

'Fay left for Sydney this morning,' he told me. 'She's got an exhibition coming up. So we'll have the place to ourselves for a couple of days. She said to say hello.'

Well that part was good news anyway. I didn't mind Dad's wife, but I was kind of glad she wasn't going to be there. Things were always a bit strained when Fay was around. She didn't have kids of her own, and I don't think she really knew how to treat me. Also, I guess she liked having Dad to herself.

Cicadas were buzzing away in the trees, but otherwise everything was very still. Then a lone police car came over the brow of the hill and cruised down the main street towards us.

'The local force on its rounds,' joked Dad.

Sunny, Elmo, Nick and Liz piled into the back of the ute, and Richelle and I squeezed into the front with Dad.

Through the dusty screen door of Skinner's General Store I could see an old woman in an apron staring at us. She didn't take her eyes off us for a minute as Dad started the engine and began to back out of his parking spot.

The police car reached us and swung into the kerb nearby. A big policeman wearing shiny sunglasses got out. He hooked his thumbs into his belt and gave us a long look as we drove by.

Seemed we were very interesting. Well, you could understand that, I thought. It was obvious that very little ever happened in Banyan.

○

Dad's new house wasn't a house at all. Well, not a proper house. It had been built as a boathouse. Dad and Fay had kept the boathouse for a living room, built a small loft upstairs for a bedroom, and put in a kitchen and bathroom. Then they'd added a larger room out one side for their studio. That was the extension we were going to paint.

The front of the house came right out to the road and the rest was on heavy poles that went down into the water. The big wooden rails that were used to pull the boats up when it was a boathouse were still there, disappearing down into the sea. Over them Dad had built a deck which was connected to a small pier. He had a rowboat tied up to one corner of the pier.

Dad opened the front door and I went in and had a quick look around.

11

'What do you think of the house?' Dad asked.

You could tell he was really proud of it.

'It looks great.'

'Great? You mean, fantastic, marvellous, stupendous, don't you? Of course you do,' he said, laughing and slapping me on the back. 'I hope your mates don't mind sleeping on mattresses on the floor.'

'No problem.'

'There's plenty of room in the studio. Fay took most of her paintings to Sydney for the exhibition and I've kind of cleared things away. Plenty of room in there.'

I knew that Richelle wouldn't like it much, but that was her bad luck. No matter how fancy it was, it would never be good enough for her.

'That'll be fine, Dad.'

Dad stepped closer and spoke in a low voice.

'Tom,' he said, 'tell your friends that it's all right to call me Mel, will you? I can't stand this "Mr Moysten" stuff.'

'Okay, Dad.'

'We should have a great time, don't you think?'

'Sure, Dad.'

We went back out to join the others. We'd just started getting the bags out of the ute when the police car cruised slowly up the track and pulled up.

'Mr Moysten?' the cop in the sunglasses said.

'At your service, Sergeant Bluett,' Dad answered.

The policeman climbed slowly out of his car and looked Dad up and down.

'Are you aware that it's an offence to ride in the back of a ute?' he said.

Liz, Sunny and I glanced at each other. Uh oh.

'Ride in the back of a ute?' Dad drawled. 'I did nothing of the kind. I was driving. Nothing against that, I hope.'

Sergeant Bluett took his sunglasses off very slowly.

'It is against the law to carry passengers in the back of a ute or to have any passengers in your vehicle who are not restrained by seat belts,' he said.

'For heaven's sake!' Dad laughed. 'We hardly went anywhere. We could have walked it.'

'Then maybe you should have,' Sergeant Bluett answered sharply. 'You haven't been in this area for long, Mr Moysten, so let me tell you this. It's an old-fashioned law-abiding community. I'm here to make sure it stays that way.'

Dad turned away and grabbed a couple of bags. 'Come on, kids,' he said casually. 'Let's get inside.'

We trailed after him into the house, resisting the temptation to look behind us. I could feel Sergeant Bluett's hard eyes watching us all the way. But Dad didn't seem worried. He pointed out the bathroom, chatted a bit to Liz about how the place used to be a boathouse, and then led us across the living room to the studio.

'Put down your stuff and then we'll have something to eat,' he said.

I cheered up a bit at that. I was ravenous.

The studio was a big, airy room with a fabulous view of the water. There were two double mattresses on the floor and two single air beds. Richelle quickly staked out her territory by throwing her bag on one of the air beds and moving it to where she'd have a view of the sea when she was lying down. Nick coolly took the other air bed.

That left one double mattress for Sunny and Liz, and one for Elmo and me. No problem. We dumped our sleeping-bags and backpacks and followed Dad back out to the living room.

Then we got a surprise. Sergeant Bluett had come inside the house and was standing there calmly sizing everything up.

'What exactly do you want, Sergeant?' Dad asked.

'Don't mind if I have a look around, do you?' The policeman didn't move, but his eyes still darted up and down the room.

'Maybe I do.' Dad was angry. You could see it.

'You don't have anything to hide, do you, Mr Moysten?'

I could feel the others fidgeting beside me. The policeman's tone was vaguely threatening. He stood there, massive in his official-looking blue uniform. Dad faced him, tall and eccentric-looking in his torn jeans and long braids. They made a strange contrast. I suddenly wished I could sketch them.

Sergeant Bluett showed his teeth in a fake smile. 'Like I said,' he went on, glancing at me and the others. 'This is a quiet little community. And we want to keep it that way.'

'Is there a point to this?' Dad drawled.

'The point, Mr Moysten, is that there are certain things this community just won't stand for. And one of those things is drugs.'

3

Drug bust

I heard Nick draw a sharp breath behind me.

'So what have drugs got to do with me, Bluett?' Dad demanded.

'You tell me, sir. Now. Do you mind if I have a look around?'

Dad made a disgusted sound. 'Oh, do what you like,' he said. He turned his back and went into the kitchen.

'If you've got a drug problem here I suggest you put the thumbscrews on some of your other law-abiding citizens,' he called out as he filled the kettle. 'Why not Elsie Skinner over at the general store? She looks pretty suspicious to me. Probably selling heroin by the biscuit tin.'

'Yes, very funny, Mr Moysten.'

Sergeant Bluett paced around the room, looking at everything. We watched him. Dad banged around in the kitchen, opening and closing the refrigerator, getting out mugs and spoons.

Six or seven of Dad's unframed paintings were stacked

16

against a wall. The policeman had a good look at the first one. It was a painting of the beach just down from the house. Wading in the water was a fat lady holding up her skirt to keep it from getting wet.

The sergeant gave a small snorting laugh and then looked through the other paintings. They were all beach scenes. One had an old couple walking along arm in arm. Another had a fisherman fishing from a small blue-and-red boat at sunset.

Sergeant Bluett pushed the stack back against the wall and looked again at the fat woman.

'Bliss Bell,' he said loudly. 'Did she know you were painting this, Mr Moysten? Did you get her permission?'

Liz, Nick and Elmo gasped. They obviously recognised the name. And I did too. Bliss Bell was a sculptor. Fairly famous. I'd had no idea she lived in Banyan Bay.

'The last time I studied the criminal code of this state it wasn't an offence to paint people,' Dad said sarcastically, without turning around. 'Or has the law been changed recently?'

Bluett looked at the painting again. 'Doesn't look much like her anyway,' he sniffed.

'No,' Dad said. 'You wouldn't recognise her in a million years, would you? Wonder how you did it?'

He'd have done better to shut up. But he couldn't help himself. I knew because I could never help myself either. Giving cheek was second nature to me. And it was always getting me into trouble. At school, with my stepfather . . .

Mouth set, the policeman strode over to the kitchen.

17

Dad didn't look at him. Bluett flicked open a cupboard and glanced at the contents. I felt myself flushing red with anger. He was acting as if Dad was no-one and nothing, and had no rights. Just because he didn't wear a suit and tie, and have a short-back-and-sides haircut.

The policeman put up a meaty hand and pulled down a large, unlabelled jar from the back of a shelf. He unscrewed the lid, and sniffed the dull green, grassy-looking stuff inside. A strange expression crossed his face. My heart jumped into my mouth.

'What's this?' he asked roughly.

'I couldn't tell you,' Dad said, barely glancing up. 'Fay does most of the cooking.'

I heard Elmo whisper something to Liz and her gasp in reply. Her hand reached for my arm and gripped it.

'Is that so?' Bluett carefully replaced the lid, screwing it tight. 'And where's your girlfriend now, Mr Moysten?'

'My *wife* is in Sydney, Sergeant,' spat Dad. 'Probably selling marijuana on the streets of Kings Cross as we speak. Got to make a living somehow, right?'

'You're not being very helpful, Mr Moysten.'

Dad's eyes were fixed on the jar in Bluett's hand. 'Just get out of here, will you?' he said quietly.

'Sure I will, Mr Moysten.' The policeman slipped the jar into his pocket. 'But I reckon I'll be back, don't you? After what's in this jar has been checked out we'll need to have another little talk. Possession of marijuana is still a serious offence. I suggest you don't leave town for a while.'

Dad's face didn't change. He didn't move a muscle.

18

He went on standing there stony-faced as the sergeant walked to the door and went out to his car.

I left the others and ran over to him. 'Dad!' I hissed at him. 'Why did you let him take it? He didn't have a search warrant. He can't . . .'

Dad just shook his head at me. He began to smile as the police car drove away.

'If there are real crims in this community they can rest easy,' he said. 'With old Bluett on the side of law and order they've got nothing to fear.' He put his hands on his hips and grinned around at our scared faces.

'Well, that was fun, wasn't it?' he said. 'But Tom's right. I shouldn't have let Bluett take the jar. We were going to have spaghetti bolognaise for dinner. And how am I going to make it without oregano?'

We sat down on the deck, looking out to sea and not saying much. Dad, Liz, Richelle and I were drinking tea. The others had glasses of mineral water or juice. The sky was blue, just starting to dim. The water was lapping at our feet. Seagulls screamed. A big white yacht rocked gently at anchor just inside the breakwater.

It should have been great. But it wasn't. The others were all stirred up. I could feel it. They felt awkward and uncomfortable. They must have been wondering what they'd got themselves into by coming to Banyan Bay. They were rattled by the place, by Dad, and by Sergeant Bluett's ridiculous drug bust.

They'd been as worried as I had about what was in that jar. For all they knew it *was* marijuana. And the way Dad had acted had fooled them as much as it had fooled Sergeant Bluett. Mind you, they had an excuse. They weren't used to Dad's sense of humour.

But I was. And I should have known Dad wouldn't have been so stupid. He might look like a hippie these days, but he's not into drugs. He doesn't even drink wine or beer much. He likes to keep his mind clear, he says.

I should have remembered that. But I guess I'd been thrown by the new house, and the plaits, and my nervousness about what the gang thought of him. In other words, I'd been a dummy. Again.

'Isn't it peaceful?' said Liz at last. Long silences always make her nervous.

'Sure is,' muttered Nick.

Silence.

'Does the surf ever get any higher than this?' asked Sunny, looking sadly at the gently heaving water of the bay.

'No—thanks to the breakwater we don't get much surf,' Dad said. 'Unless there's a big storm.'

'That's a shame,' Richelle said, putting into words what everyone else was thinking.

'Not as far as I'm concerned,' Dad grinned, sipping at his tea. 'Big waves have an annoying habit of washing houses like this into the drink.'

'I love the sound of waves,' Liz said. 'I hope it'll storm

while we're here.'

Dad rubbed his chin. 'It might,' he told her. 'And if you love the sound of waves you're in the right place here, Liz. It's wonderful to lie in bed at night, hearing them crash into the poles under the house, wondering if the whole place is going to sink to the bottom of the bay. Fay and I love it. We often stay awake all night, thinking about it.'

Nick laughed. Liz blushed. Dad hadn't meant to, but he'd made her feel silly.

Silence. Dad sat for a moment more, then muttered something about a phone call and went inside. I think he'd realised that we'd get on better without him. I felt sorry about that. He wanted everyone to feel comfortable with him. He wanted us to think of him as just another kid. But of course we couldn't. Especially me.

As soon as he'd gone, I felt the gang relax. They lay back, stretched out their legs, gradually began to chat. I felt myself relaxing too. I hadn't realised this visit would be such a strain. I hoped the whole week wouldn't be the same.

After a while, the faint sound of music began drifting to us across the water from the yacht. A man in a white jacket appeared on the stern and threw a bucket of scraps into the sea. Seagulls plunged down screaming to pick up bits and pieces, then soared off towards the headland beyond.

'Tough life, living on a yacht, huh?' I said.

'Yeah,' agreed Elmo. 'All that stress. Worrying about where to sail next. What to get the cook to make for dinner.'

'Which dress to wear to which party. Too exhausting for words, daaarling,' Liz said with a sigh. 'I couldn't stand the pressure.'

'I think I could cope,' said Nick.

Silence. But this time the silence was calm instead of tense.

I felt myself lulled by the sound of the lapping water. I looked around the bay. The yacht swayed gently in the light breeze. A few people walked on the little beach. Seagulls flew for the headland. A fisherman sat in a blue-and-red fishing boat with his line in the water. It was the man from Dad's painting. As I watched he pulled in a fish. He re-baited the hook and threw the line in again. He caught another fish.

I watched on, fascinated. Would he catch a third? How long would it take him?

'What are you staring at, Tom?' Sunny asked curiously. 'What's so interesting about that fisherman?'

'He's catching fish,' I told her.

'Wow, Tom, that's thrilling!' teased Liz.

I laughed. It looked like Banyan Bay was getting to me already. If someone had told me yesterday that I could spend ten minutes watching a man fish, I'd have said they were crazy. But I'd just done it. And I'd enjoyed it, too.

'Let's keep the thrills going,' drawled Nick. 'Let's go down to the beach. We might find a dead crab. Or see a car go down the main street or something.'

Even Nick couldn't spoil my new relaxed mood. I grinned at him as I hauled myself to my feet. 'You never know your luck,' I said. 'But let's walk slowly. We don't want to get overexcited.'

Dad was talking on the phone as we walked back through the living room. He nodded as I pointed and mimed to tell him where we were going. Then he put his hand over the mouthpiece and spoke to us.

'Have a good time, gang,' he said. 'Enjoy the last of your freedom. Tomorrow it's hard labour day. House painting from sunup to sunset.'

Everyone laughed nervously. They still weren't quite sure about Dad.

'Oh, and Tom,' he added, 'on your way back could you call into the shop and get some oregano? Somehow I don't think I'll be getting mine back for a while.'

4

Beach bound

The beach was lined with little houses that looked straight out to the bay. The main road, if you could call it that, ran along behind them. In front of most of the houses was a small rowboat, pulled up in the low dunes. Each boat was tied with a long line to concrete blocks to keep it from being washed away in a storm.

We walked along the tideline, Nick again telling his puzzle. All of us were listening except Richelle, who was walking on ahead.

'Okay,' he said. 'Three dollars each. Their friend gets the ball for two-fifty.'

'Did he get his change as one fifty-cent coin?' Sunny asked.

'It doesn't matter,' Nick answered. 'But let's say he got back one twenty-cent coin and three ten-cent coins. So he gave the guys each ten cents and kept the twenty-cent piece for himself.'

'So they each paid a dollar and got ten cents back,'

Elmo said.

'Right. So they each paid ninety cents for the cricket ball. Three times ninety is two dollars seventy, isn't it?'

We all agreed that it was.

'And that's what they think their friend paid. But he didn't, he only paid two dollars fifty. He pocketed the extra twenty cents. So two dollars seventy plus the twenty cents in his pocket is two dollars ninety. Where's the other ten cents?'

'Maybe he dropped it on the way home,' Sunny said.

Everyone groaned.

'Sunny, come on,' Nick said. 'That's got nothing to do with it.'

'Why not?'

'Because there wasn't any ten cents.'

'But you said what happened to it?'

'That's the whole point.'

'Then I solved the puzzle, did I?'

'Sunny, just forget it,' Nick asked.

Richelle turned back.

'Is that that cricket-ball puzzle?' she asked. 'Could somebody tell it to me?'

'Rich,' Nick said. 'Forget it.'

Liz and I were walking behind the others. An old couple passed us, going in the other direction, walking arm in arm. They nodded as they passed and we said hello. They looked like they were a hundred years old and had been married for eighty. I guess that was what made Liz start thinking about Dad and Fay.

'What's Fay like?' she asked.

'Oh, she's okay.'

'Okay?'

'She's really good.'

'Good?'

'She's a really good painter. Dad reckons she's better than he is.'

I didn't want to talk about Fay. She was all right, but I was glad she was away.

'It must be strange having a stepmother,' Liz said.

'Yeah,' I said.

Actually I never thought of Fay as being my stepmother or Brian as being my stepfather. To me, Brian was Mum's husband and Fay was Dad's wife. Mother and father never came into it.

I stopped and started throwing bits of shell into the water. The old couple were still toddling on up the beach, arm in arm.

'You know they're only twenty-five years old,' I whispered to Liz. 'Twenty-five years in Banyan Bay and you'd look like that too.'

'I think Banyan Bay's pretty,' Liz said.

'Pretty creepy, if you ask me.'

'Rubbish.'

'It's got great views, but there's something wrong here. I can't put my finger on it. Everything looks normal, but it's got bad vibes.'

'Since when did you believe in vibes?'

'Since we got here.'

It was true: something about Banyan gave me the creeps. It wasn't just Nuk Nuk without the tourists and the shops and the surf. There was something else, something deeper. It was as though the place wasn't right. It was like a place where mass murderers went on holidays.

'That policeman was really off,' Liz said. 'I thought your dad was great the way he stood up to him.'

'Dad's good at standing up people. He doesn't like taking orders from anybody.'

'That's good.'

'It wasn't so good when he was an architect. Mum reckons he never wanted to build people's houses the way they wanted them built. He always had *better* ways. It's hard to get your own way when someone else is paying for it.'

Ahead of us, Nick had pulled a long piece of seaweed out of the water and was swinging it around his head, chasing Richelle. Richelle screamed as she ran, wrapping her arms around her head to keep from getting sand and water in her hair.

Up ahead, the fisherman I'd seen from Dad's deck pulled his boat up onto the beach. It had a small outboard motor which he'd pulled up so the propeller wouldn't scrape the sand.

He wore scruffy old clothes and a big straw hat. His grizzled beard looked like it hadn't been combed for years.

'Who does that guy look like to you?' I asked Liz.

'Space Man. You know, that guy we see on Wattle Street. The one who keeps raving on about spaceships landing and everything.'

'No. This guy doesn't look as off the air as Space Man. I reckon he looks like the Old Man from *The Old Man and the Sea*.'

'Who?'

'It's a book. And a movie too, I think. It's about a man who catches a giant fish that tows him way out to sea. It nearly kills him, but he won't give up.'

But Liz had stopped listening. She was peering at a sort of shed next to one of the houses that lined the beachfront. 'Hey, that's her!' she whispered, clutching my arm excitedly.

Inside the shed was a very fat woman working with some clay. She stood there in bare feet with a huge piece of cloth wound around her for a dress. Heavy black hair, streaked with grey, fell down her back almost to her knees.

'Imagine that!' breathed Liz. 'Bliss Bell!'

5

Fatty and Skinny

Liz ran forward and stopped the others. 'Bliss Bell,' I heard her whispering to them.

So what? I thought. But the others were interested. Maybe Banyan Bay was getting to them, too. They started edging up into the dunes in a cluster, trying to get a closer look.

Bliss Bell's house was painted a faded pink. It had a rusty iron roof. There was nothing in the garden but dune grass and a few scrubby bushes. The houses on either side of hers looked like they'd been abandoned for years. Their windows were all broken and there was a big hole in the roof of one of them.

'I wonder why she doesn't do more with her house? I'll bet she's rich,' Richelle whispered.

'Don't be so sure,' I answered.

I knew that Dad and Fay worked really hard at their paintings, and they barely made a living. They were lucky if they sold a painting a month and then half the money went to the gallery that sold it, and a lot of the rest went for picture frames and shipping the paintings around.

'But she's famous,' Richelle protested. 'Liz said so.'

'That doesn't mean anything,' I said. 'Lots of people are famous and they don't make much money.'

'She's so poor,' Nick said, 'that she can't afford clothes. She has to wear curtains.'

'It's not a curtain, stupid,' Richelle snapped. 'It's a sarong.' She looked again at Bliss Bell. 'Still,' she said disapprovingly. 'It may as well be a curtain. It looks awful.'

Just at that moment Bliss Bell turned around and saw us watching her. She frowned furiously.

'Hey you!' she roared, running forward like a charging rhino and shaking a clay-stained fist at us. 'You kids! Get out of there before I call the police!'

We all got such a shock that we just took off, pelting back down the dunes and along the beach. A few metres on I tripped over my own feet in the soft sand and did a complete somersault, landing flat on my bottom. Of course the others thought that was the funniest thing they'd ever seen. They started shrieking and giggling like a lot of little kids.

'See how much fun this place is?' hooted Liz, hauling me up with tears running down her cheeks.

'Yeah,' I growled. 'It's a laugh a minute. For some.'

We set off for the store, but we hadn't gone far before Liz

said, 'I think I'm about to have an art attack.'

'A *what?*' groaned Sunny.

'An *art* attack,' grinned Liz, pleased by her own cleverness. 'Everyone's painting paintings and sculpting sculptures around here. It makes me want to do something arty too. I think I'll make a collage to remind me of Banyan Bay.'

'Couldn't you just take a photograph?' sighed Nick.

But Liz had the fire of a new project in her eyes. She spent the rest of the walk to Skinner's General Store bent double, picking up things from the tideline.

By the time we got to the shop she was holding the bottom of her T-shirt out to carry her collection of wood, shells, feathers, dry seaweed, smooth pieces of glass, a dead starfish, pretty coloured stones and the odd sweet wrapper.

My Old Man of the Sea was already at the shop, talking to Mrs Skinner. Well, Mrs Skinner was doing all the talking. All the poor guy wanted was some milk and a newspaper, but she wasn't going to let him out of the place till she'd said everything she wanted to say.

'The way things are today,' she croaked, 'you can't afford to do anything. The rates are so high on this place! It's criminal! And what do I get for my money? Nothing. Rubbish removal? Don't make me laugh. Half the time they forget to come. And what else? One useless copper and a fire brigade that couldn't put out a match in a shower.'

The fisherman rumbled something, and waited patiently for his change. You got the feeling that he'd heard all this before.

Mrs Skinner was truly *very* skinny. She wore an old apron and fluffy slippers and she had a red-tipped nose and beady eyes that made her look like an eagle. Her high, whining voice went on and on. She didn't take any notice of us, hanging around behind the fisherman. We wouldn't make much of an audience. And she wanted to get a few things off her chest.

'Was a time when Banyan Bay was a thriving little community. You know that?' she shrilled. 'But they've let it go, and let it go, and now look! Dead and may as well be buried. I wouldn't have more than five or six customers in a day, these days. Criminal!'

She drew breath, and the fisherman held out his hand hopefully. She plonked his change down and pursed her lips.

'You know what makes me *really* cranky?' she demanded. She didn't get an answer, but she didn't need one. She was going to tell him anyway.

'Those yachts!' she snapped. 'Big, fancy things, coming into our bay to get out of the rough seas. A good safe mooring for free. But do they shop here? Put a bit of money back into the town? Not on your life. Soon as they're good and ready they're off again, to buy up big in Bentone or Nuk Nuk. Never mind poor old Banyan Bay. We're not posh enough for them!'

'Well, I'd better be off,' the Old Man of the Sea said, edging for the door.

As soon as he left the shop Mrs Skinner turned her

fierce little eyes onto us.

'What do you kids want?' she asked sharply.

We were all just kind of looking around, but Nick and Richelle were having a laugh about some of the dusty old things they'd found on the shelves. I guess she'd seen them.

'Could I have some oregano, please?' I asked.

'No. We don't have it,' she snapped. 'No point. Who'd buy it, round here?'

'We would, for starters,' Nick pointed out.

She glared at him. 'Oh, is that right? Well if you want fancy stuff like that you'll have to go up to Nuk Nuk for it.'

Nick turned away, shaking his head. 'What a way to run a business,' he muttered.

Mrs Skinner heard him. She leaned across the counter, her eyes like little black stones. 'I'll have you know, boy, that my father started this shop fifty years ago,' she called after him. 'I know my business. It's a good old-fashioned place, the Bay. We don't go in for all that la-di-da stuff—just the necessities.'

'But we *need* oregano,' I said. 'For us *it's* a necessity. Have you ever had spaghetti sauce without oregano?'

'Plenty of tinned spaghetti down the back,' snapped Mrs Skinner.

Beside the counter was a curtained doorway that led back into Mrs Skinner's house—well, the rooms she lived in at the back of the shop.

I heard a slight noise from somewhere behind there. I glanced through the gap between the curtains and into the darkened hallway beyond just in time to see a black shape

33

step quickly to one side, back into hiding. I drew a quick breath. Someone had been watching us!

Quick as a flash Mrs Skinner pulled the curtains shut and glared furiously at me.

I pretended I hadn't seen anything, and turned away. But my mind was racing. Who was behind the curtain? Why were they hiding? How long had they been there?

Liz had managed to pick up a small bottle of glue from a shelf while still holding her T-shirt in both hands. She came forward to the counter.

'Is this the only glue you have?' she asked.

'What's wrong with it?' Mrs Skinner demanded, still casting black looks in my direction.

'I'm making a collage. I want to stick these thing down with it,' Liz explained. 'I don't think this is strong enough.'

'Well, it's all we have. Take it or leave it.'

Liz decided to take it. She didn't have any choice.

Nick had the fridge door open and was picking up everything, looking it over and then putting it back.

'I thought I'd buy some nice cheese for your dad,' he said to me. 'But there's only this ordinary stuff, and the kind with the little individual slices.'

Mrs Skinner gave Liz her glue and her change, and looked the rest of us over like we were a gang of shoplifters.

'Are you kids going to buy anything else, or not?' she muttered.

'We'd like to,' Nick said coolly, 'but there's so little to buy. Guess we'll have to go down to Bentone or up to Nuk Nuk to stock up. Like the people on the yachts.'

'That'd be right,' snarled Mrs Skinner in disgust.

'You could try keeping things that people on holiday actually want to buy, you know,' said Nick.

If Mrs Skinner had been in a cartoon, smoke would have poured out of her ears. She looked like she was going to explode. But she didn't say a word to Nick. Instead she turned to me.

'What did Bluett want at your place?' she snapped.

'I—I don't know,' I blurted out, taken by surprise.

'He just came to borrow some oregano,' Nick chipped in. 'He couldn't find any for sale.'

'You get out of here, you young smart alec,' Mrs Skinner yelled, shaking a bony finger at Nick. 'I've had enough of you.'

We shuffled out of the shop. The others were smothering giggles, but I was thoughtful.

Mrs Skinner's shop wasn't everything it seemed. And neither was Mrs Skinner. She was hiding something.

Someone had been watching us from the dark corridor behind her shop. Someone who didn't want us to know of their existence.

Like the rest of Banyan Bay, Skinner's General Store was guarding a secret. I could feel it.

6

Skeletons in
the closet

The sun was setting. The hundred-year-old couple sat on their veranda, muttering to each other and watching us as we walked past. The Old Man of the Sea was standing beside his boat, sorting out his fishing gear.

'I could go for a good piece of John Dory,' Nick said.

'Not me,' Richelle said. 'I hate fish.'

'How can you hate fish? Fish are beautiful.'

'They're awful—yuck! Just the way they look. They look dead even when they're alive,' Richelle said. 'And they're full of bones.'

'Bones? You just have to know how to eat them, that's all.'

'The bones get stuck in your throat. They can kill you. You know the Queen?'

'Not personally,' Nick answered.

'Well, they say her mother, the Queen Mother, used to

get bones stuck in her throat every time she ate fish. They had to keep rushing her off to hospital. Every time they had fish at the palace, they had an ambulance standing by ready to whip her into hospital.'

'That's bull,' Sunny said.

'No, it's true,' Richelle insisted. 'It's *true!*'

'Dad says that if you get a bone in your throat you're supposed to eat a big chunk of bread to push it down,' said Elmo.

'What if it doesn't push it down but it pushes it through your throat and right into your heart?' Richelle asked.

There wasn't much of an answer to that one, but Sunny tried. 'I don't really think that's possible, Richelle,' she said.

'Well, whether it is or it isn't, it doesn't matter to me,' said Richelle calmly. 'All that matters to me is, I don't like fish.'

❁

Guess what we had for dinner? Bad luck, Richelle.

Well, Dad thought some freshly-caught fish would be a treat for us. And spag bol was off the menu, at least till he could get to Nuk Nuk and a new supply of oregano. So he'd bought seven nice little fishies from a couple of the fishermen down the beach. Not the Old Man of the Sea, he told me. Harry never sold his fish. He froze them for a rainy day, and to give away to townie friends. Must have a freezer-full by now, Dad said enviously. Dad loves fish.

Anyway, he'd gutted the fish he'd bought and barbecued them whole—eyes and all. I thought Richelle was going to be sick when she got her first look at her plate. I have to admit I wasn't too keen on the look of those dead eyes myself. But the fish tasted wonderful. It melted in your mouth.

We sat around a tablecloth on the floor to eat. There were cushions on the floor for chairs.

I hate sitting on the floor because my legs go to sleep after about two seconds. But nobody else seemed to mind.

Dad kept asking if everybody liked the meal, so Richelle had to pretend she loved it. We all put pieces of bread next to her plate till there was a huge pile of it. Dad didn't get the joke, of course.

When Richelle finished eating there were wads of chewed up fish and bones on her plate—like she'd had to spit out practically every mouthful because she couldn't get the bones out.

Nick's plate was just the opposite: a neat fish skeleton and a pile of bones without a piece of fish on them.

'How'd you get on with Elsie Skinner?' Dad asked.

'I think we convinced her to turn her place into a gourmet deli,' Nick grinned.

'That'll be the day.'

'She didn't like us much,' said Liz, with her mouth full.

'I don't think she likes anyone very much,' said Elmo. 'But boy, she can talk. She earbashed that poor fisherman all right, didn't she?'

They laughed. But I frowned. I was remembering the person in the dark corridor.

'Elsie's problem,' Dad said, 'is that she's lonely. She lives alone and she doesn't have anyone to talk to except people who come into the shop. But she knows everything there is to know about Banyan. Collects gossip like a spider collects flies. And if you think she doesn't like you, wait till you hear her on the subject of Bliss Bell.'

'Why Bliss Bell?' Liz asked.

'They've got this feud going. Elsie was furious when Bliss bought the two houses on either side of her own place.'

'The ones that are falling down?'

'Too right. Bliss bought them to give herself more privacy. She didn't want nosy neighbours.'

'What does Mrs Skinner care?' Liz was leaning forward, very interested. She loves stories about people.

'Two less families in town to buy groceries from Skinner's store,' Dad explained. 'But their feud goes back a lot further than that. There was something about Elsie's son, Andy. He was a real problem when he was a teenager, apparently.'

He put his knife and fork together and pushed his plate away from him with a contented sigh. 'Boy, that was good,' he said.

'What happened?' Liz persisted. 'About Andy and Bliss Bell?'

'Oh, Bliss caught him prowling around her place one night,' Dad shrugged. 'She reckoned he was trying to break in. He probably was. She got the cops to warn him off, and he finished up leaving town. Elsie hasn't spoken to Bliss from that day to this.'

'It's a good old-fashioned place, the Bay,' Liz laughed. Her eyes were sparkling.

A good old-fashioned place. Sure! I thought. Our first idea of peaceful, friendly Banyan Bay was a joke. Sergeant Bluett, Elsie Skinner and Bliss Bell had been about as rude and suspicious as anyone could be. This place made Raven Hill seem like the love-thy-neighbour capital of the world.

After the dinner things were cleared away, I got out my sketchbook and started drawing people, partly realistic, partly caricature. Since we were in the land of opposites, I made them the opposites of what they seemed to be.

The first sketch I didn't have to make up. It was a drawing of Dad as he used to look when he worked as an architect in an office. I gave him a neat polo neck skivvy, short hair and a pencil behind his ear.

Then I did one of the man with the boat—Harry, the Old Man of the Sea—only I took away his wild beard and put him in a suit, with a tie and a briefcase, and a bottle of mineral water.

I did one of Richelle with her hair in curlers and wearing a daggy quilted dressing-gown and fluffy slippers like Mrs Skinner's. Then I made Mrs Skinner an elegant, rich lady in an evening dress, wearing earrings and a big diamond necklace.

What was Liz's opposite? At first I didn't know.

I studied her as she worked on her collage. All the shells and bits of driftwood and everything lay in neat little piles on the floor. Dad had given her a piece of canvas board to stick them on.

Liz is hard-working, enthusiastic about things, and soft-hearted. She's also a bit shy, really, behind all that chatter she goes on with. I made her a real rager. She was dancing on a piano at a party wearing a bikini and high heels and a fluffy feather stole.

Nick, Mr Cool, I drew as a real ocker in thongs and shorts and a little towelling hat. Then I put him in a barbecue apron with 'Kiss the Cook' written on it, and gave him a sausage on a long fork to hold. I enjoyed that.

I put Sunny on a couch watching TV and eating chocolates. I'll bet she's never done such a thing in her life. Her idea of taking it easy is running once around the block instead of twice.

I was having fun drawing Elmo, grinning in a dinner suit with his curly hair all slicked back and a microphone in his hand, when Dad came and looked over my shoulder.

'Opposites,' he said, getting the point straightaway. 'That's clever. Really clever, Tom.'

He meant it. I was very pleased. I knew he wouldn't say my work was good if it wasn't. I let him take my sketchbook from me and flick back through the pages. 'You always do people or animals,' he commented, handing it back. 'What about landscapes?'

'I do them sometimes, too,' I said. 'But I'm into people right now.'

Dad nodded. 'People are tricky, of course,' he said. 'If you make a painting look just like them they usually hate

41

it. It's safer to paint landscapes. Then nobody wants to sue you.'

Liz looked over my shoulder at the drawing I'd done of her.

'Hey, what's this?' she shrieked. 'Give me that, you rat!'

I clutched it to my chest to keep her from getting it.

Dad laughed. 'See what I mean?'

7

The rising tide

That night I lay in my sleeping-bag listening to the wind and the water outside as the others slept peacefully around me.

I couldn't sleep. I didn't think I'd ever get to sleep again.

It had been a fun evening. Everyone seemed to have relaxed, and got to understand that Dad wasn't as weird as he looked. He'd relaxed too. He'd stopped trying to be one of the gang, and started just being himself. Which was nice.

But now all the laughing and chat had stopped. The lights were out. Everyone was asleep. So I was alone with my thoughts. And I kept thinking of the sea, lapping away at the poles underneath me. I imagined the house slowly slipping into the water with us trapped inside.

I remembered seeing a TV documentary about finding this huge passenger ship on the bottom of the ocean floor. I think it was the *Titanic* or something. They sent cameras down first and then they lowered a couple of guys down in one of those tiny steel submarines that was suspended from a cable.

In the powerful lights you could just make out the rusting deck of the ship lying upright in the mud. There was a long tear in one side where it had scraped an iceberg.

The program kept going on about all the valuable paintings and jewellery that were still in the ship, but all I could think of were the passengers who'd gone down in it.

The sea. You can have it.

●

I must have gone to sleep in the end, because when I opened my eyes sun was streaming into the studio straight into my face. I looked around me. Everyone else was still dead to the world.

Last night's horror was just a nasty memory. I got up and grabbed my sketchbook. Sliding the glass door open I stepped out onto the deck to see the sights of the bay in the morning light.

The Old Man of the Sea was already out in his favourite spot, pulling in fish. The water was rippling and bubbling around the boat as if a whole school of fish were in a frenzy below, waiting to throw themselves at his hook. Some people have all the luck.

I made a drawing of him, trying to get the feeling of motion, him pulling on his line, the bubbles in the water, a seagull swooping down. I put in lots of action lines.

When I'd finished, I went into the living room and found Dad's painting of the same man. Dad's colours were good and his brushwork was good but there was something I didn't like about it. Maybe it was because there was no movement in the painting at all. It was still, like a bowl of fruit on a table or like a photograph. I could see that it was good, but it wasn't the kind of thing that I'd ever do, even if I learnt to paint as well as Dad.

Maybe that was the difference between Dad and me, I thought. Dad was happy and peaceful living with Fay, living down here in Banyan, looking at the sea. If he suddenly won a million dollars he'd probably just stay here and do what he liked to do: go for walks, go fishing, paint—or just do nothing at all. Dad had found his comfortable place in life.

I knew I wasn't like that. I'm the jumpy and fidgety type. If I won a million dollars I'd probably work myself into a nervous breakdown searching for ways to spend the money.

'Not bad, is it?' Liz yawned.

I turned to find her looking over my shoulder at Dad's painting.

'This is my version,' I said, showing her my sketch.

'What are these lines beside his arm?'

'He was pulling in fish.'

Liz looked at my sketch with her head on one side. 'It's not bad, either,' she said finally. 'In fact, it's really good. But it's very different, isn't it?'

I looked at the two pictures side by side. One smooth,

still, and finished. One sketchy, energetic, and raw.

'Yes,' I sighed, 'very different.'

○

'Now let me get this straight,' Dad said. 'They all pay one dollar, so that makes three dollars in all. The other guy buys the cricket ball for two-fifty. He gives them back ten cents each and keeps twenty.'

'Right,' said Elmo. 'Three times ninety is two dollars seventy. Add the twenty cents he took out and that's two dollars ninety. What happened to the other ten cents?'

Dad had two frying pans on the stove. He was cooking eggs and bacon, trying to make toast, and working on Nick's puzzle all at the same time.

'I'll have to give that one some thought,' he said.

I knew he was just stalling. Dad isn't the puzzle type.

Neither is Richelle. But she wasn't listening anyway. She was reading her *Simply Stylish* magazine.

'Liz, look at these *gorgeous* Dixie lamps,' she drooled.

'Let's see.'

'What's a Dixie lamp?' asked Elmo.

Richelle sighed at his ignorance and showed him—and then the rest of us—the Dixie lamps in her magazine. They were truly horrible: lamps in the shapes of animals dressed up like people.

One was a sheep sitting up wearing a tartan vest with the light fitting coming out from between its horns. Another one was two koalas in board shorts standing arm

46

in arm. There was a cow wearing an apron and standing on her hind legs, smiling, and a hippopotamus in a pink bonnet and shawl.

'Aren't they so *cute!*' shrieked Richelle.

Sunny snorted in disgust.

'Yeah, they're nice,' Liz said.

'Liz, what's wrong with you?' said Nick. 'They're *awful*. They're gross. I wouldn't give you fifty cents for one.'

'Fifty cents?' Richelle said. 'Do you *know* how much they cost?'

'What does that matter?'

'Just guess.'

Nick took the magazine and had a closer look.

'A hundred bucks,' he said.

'And the rest,' sniffed Richelle. 'For your information, they cost between five hundred and a thousand dollars.'

Nick gaped at the pictures in front of him. 'You're joking!' he said finally.

'Wish I was,' said Richelle. 'I'd adore one. But I can't afford it.'

Dad brought over some plates of eggs and bacon. Everyone fell on them. For the moment, Dixie lamps and money were forgotten in favour of breakfast.

'Have you worked out the puzzle yet?' Elmo asked Dad.

He shook his head. 'Don't call me, I'll call you,' he joked.

'Hey, were you telling that puzzle again?' Richelle asked Elmo. 'Why do you always leave me out? Why don't you tell me, too?'

'Later, Richelle,' Elmo said. 'I'm all puzzled out.'

○

After breakfast, I washed the dishes, Liz, Elmo and Sunny dried and Nick stacked the stuff away. Richelle sat on a stool nearby painting her fingernails bright pink. As she explained, the kitchen was too small to have too many people working in it at one time, so she'd keep out of the way. Somehow she made it sound as though she was doing us a favour.

Dad was just getting everything ready so we could start painting the outside of the studio, when the phone rang.

He answered it. And suddenly he looked frightened.

'Yes, she's my wife,' he said loudly. 'Yes . . . yes . . . Are you sure? . . . I'll be there as soon as I can. I'm in Banyan Bay. Could be four or five hours.'

He was shaking when he put the phone down.

'It's Fay,' he whispered. 'She's been in a car accident. She's in hospital.'

'Is she going to be okay?' The words rushed out of me before I could stop them.

He forced a smile. 'She's serious but not critical, they said. Whatever that means. But look, I've got to go. I've got to go now. You understand, don't you? Will you be okay on your own for a night?'

'Of course we will,' exclaimed Liz. 'Just go. We'll be fine.'

The others just stared. No-one knew what to say.

Dad started towards the stairs to the loft but then turned around and headed straight for the front door. I could tell he wasn't himself. I followed him out to the ute.

'Are you okay to drive?' I asked, touching his arm through the window.

'I'm okay,' he said. 'Fay's going to be okay. Everything's going to be okay.'

I gripped his arm more tightly, and he seemed to pull himself together a bit. 'Sorry about this, Tom,' he muttered. 'I'll ring tonight. Just buy anything you need from the shop. Sorry, I've only got enough cash for petrol. You'll have to get Elsie Skinner to put it on my bill.'

He started the engine. I let go of his arm. In the state he was in he was quite capable of driving off with my hand attached.

'Which hospital did they take Fay to, Dad?'

'St Vincent's,' he yelled, over the sound of the engine. 'Bye! Don't worry about the painting. We'll do it later. Don't worry about anything. Everything's going to be okay.'

He spun the wheel, turned the ute and roared away with a shriek of tyres. He was going too fast. I hoped Sergeant Bluett wasn't hanging around. I hoped Dad wouldn't have an accident himself on the way to Sydney.

Mum always said that Dad wasn't good under pressure, and I guess this proved it. But wouldn't anyone have panicked if his wife had been in a car crash and he didn't know how she was?

Was she really going to be all right? Or were they just

saying that? I crossed my fingers. I didn't really care much
about Fay one way or the other. But Dad did. And I cared
about him. For his sake, I hoped against hope that
everything really *would* be okay.

○

'So what are we going to do now?' Sunny asked, after we'd
finished the washing up. 'We can't just sit around here.'

'I don't see why not,' yawned Richelle, admiring her
newly-painted fingernails. 'What is there to do anyway?'

'When in Banyan Bay,' Nick said, 'do as the Banyan
Bayers do. Go fishing.'

'Yes!' cried Liz. 'That'd be great! And we might catch
our own dinner and save some money. Your dad won't
mind if we take the boat out will he, Tom?'

'No, of course not,' I said slowly. 'But wouldn't you
rather go for a walk?'

'No way,' Nick said. 'I can walk at home. Who's
coming? How about you, Richelle? Feel like some more
little fishy wishies for din dins?'

Richelle sighed heavily, and ignored him.

'They say rowing's awfully good for your figure,' said
Liz slyly. She hadn't known Richelle since pre-school for
nothing.

Richelle flicked back her hair. 'I like rowing,' she said.
She stretched out her long legs. 'Oh, well, we may as well
go. Nothing else to do.'

I knew it was hopeless, then. We were going to go

fishing. Richelle had spoken.

I told them that I wanted to do some sketching, but they wouldn't let me stay behind. I guess I could have—and should have—insisted. But I didn't know what was going to happen. And I didn't want them to know I was scared.

8

A little accident

Dad's boat was just a little rowboat. The six of us barely squeezed into it.

We started off with Elmo and Sunny rowing, but Sunny was so much stronger that we kept going in circles. Richelle took Elmo's place and—surprise surprise—she did really well. Who would have thought that glam-puss Richelle would know how to row a boat?

'Try not to break a fingernail,' Nick warned her. 'I'd hate to be stuck out here because of a broken fingernail.'

'Very funny.'

Dad's and Fay's fishing lines were tangled together and it took Liz about ten minutes of careful work to get them apart. Then she and Elmo put some smelly old bait from the bucket on the hooks and began fishing.

We all took turns, but after an hour none of us had even had a nibble. Liz and Sunny changed places. Richelle stayed where she was. I think she rather liked having control of the oars.

We rowed to a new spot, nearer to the shore, but still there was no sign of a fish.

'I think the Old Man of the Sea caught every last one of them,' Liz said after a while. 'Or maybe this bait's no good.'

'I'm just being selective,' nodded Elmo. 'I'm holding out for a tuna or a black marlin.'

'I reckon that guy knows something we don't know,' Sunny said. 'There's probably only one place in the bay you can possibly catch anything and he's sitting on top of it.'

'He's the Old Man of the Sea,' I told her. 'He's at one with the deep. You and Elmo are definitely at two with the deep.'

The boat rose and fell as the deep water moved slowly underneath us. I tried not to think about it.

Richelle looked back at the house.

'Hey, Tom, your dad's back,' she said.

We all peered in the direction she was pointing.

'I can't see him,' I said.

'He was looking out the window,' she insisted. 'I'm sure he was.'

'But his car's not there,' Sunny pointed out. 'If it was we could see it where he parks it next to that tree.'

'That's funny,' Richelle said.

'Hilarious,' drawled Nick. 'Hey, hand over that line, Sunny. It's my turn.'

I stretched out with my legs under the middle seat so I could lie back against the side of the boat and close my eyes. I thought this would cure my jitters. Instead it had the opposite effect.

'What do you say we head in now?' I said, finally.

'Come on, Tom,' Nick said. 'There's a whole school of bream heading our way. I'm using my mental sonar. *Blip blip blip blip*. Coming closer. Let's stay here a few more minutes.'

The image of a huge school of fish moving together under the water sent my mind back to the ship at the bottom of the sea. The skull of a drowned man stared blankly upwards, grinning towards the water's surface kilometres above. A sea snake slithered though the mud.

I was breathing quickly now. I opened my eyes again and forced a smile.

'Did you know that "flake" is really shark?' Sunny said. 'Like when you buy flake in a fish shop it's really shark? Sometimes when you get fish and chips you get shark.'

'Why don't they call it shark, then?' Richelle asked.

'If they called it shark no-one would buy it. Would you eat it if you knew it was shark?'

'I wouldn't eat it if it was barramundi stuffed with gold,' Richelle said.

'Would someone please throw that girl overboard?' Nick growled. 'She's driving the fish away. They can tell she doesn't like them. She's jinxing our mission!'

He threw down his line, stood up and grabbed Richelle around the waist, rocking her backwards and forwards as if he was trying to get her to stand up. She clutched at the seat with both hands.

'Get your hands off me! Let me go!'

'Nick, stop it!' shouted Liz. 'Don't be stupid! Sit down!'

The boat was rocking wildly now and I held on for dear life, feeling sick to my stomach, hoping they'd stop.

'Nick, sit *down*!' Liz shrieked.

'Oh, so you want to go for a swim too, do you?' Nick grinned. He grabbed Liz by the arms and pulled her to her feet. The two of them were standing in the middle of the boat, struggling. I worked my legs out from under the seat. The last thing I wanted was to be trapped if the boat went over.

'Hey! Cut it out!' I screamed. 'Stop mucking around, Nick! Just stop it!'

Nick and Liz went still and everyone looked at me, surprised at how upset I was.

I licked my lips. 'Sit down,' I said, trying to keep my voice from trembling. 'You shouldn't ever play the fool in a boat. It's not safe.'

Nick started to say something, but then he must have seen his fishing line move because he suddenly dived back into his seat in the bow, grabbed the line and started pulling it in.

'Hey! I've got something!' he yelled. 'I've caught a fish—and it's huge!'

He stood up, pulling harder and harder at the line. Circles of it fell, dripping, to the floor of the boat. Sunny and Elmo crowded in closer to me, peering over Liz's head to see. The boat dipped, and water came splashing over the side, onto my lap. I gasped and half-stood.

55

And at that exact moment, the line snapped. Nick fell crashing to the floor of the boat, rocking it wildly. And I overbalanced and went plunging over the side and into the water.

There was a shock of cold and for a minute I found myself thrashing around helplessly, wondering which way was up.

Finally my head broke through the surface. Air! I gasped greedily, coughed, and looked for the boat. It was just a few metres away.

Everyone was looking down at me and laughing. I tried to grin back, weak with relief. I saw that they'd changed places. Nick had taken the oars. Richelle was in the bow. Sunny, Liz and Elmo were in the stern.

'You okay?' called Liz.

I coughed a couple of times but tried to stay calm.

'I'm okay,' I said. 'Just bring the boat over, Nick.'

'It's better with just the five of us,' he said. 'We've decided to go into the beach. Get a drink at the shop, maybe. I think you should swim home.'

I was treading water, moving my hands back and forth furiously to keep my head above water.

'Well?' grinned Nick.

I took a couple of strokes towards the boat, but when I put my head up again he'd moved the boat away.

'You need some exercise,' he yelled. 'You're too slack, Moysten.'

I managed a couple more strokes, and then two more, but every time I got close, Nick pulled harder, making the boat move away from me again.

I stopped and caught my breath.

'Cut it out,' I gasped. 'Come on, Nick.'

I wanted to tell them that I was a hopeless swimmer, but I couldn't—I just couldn't.

'What's wrong, Tom?' Elmo laughed. 'We're waiting.'

'Are you sure you're okay?' Sunny asked.

Before I could say no, Nick dug the oars in deep and the boat shot forwards. Another few strokes and it had caught a small swell that sent it speeding in towards the beach.

I paddled slowly after them, struggling to keep afloat. I could feel the strength draining from my arms. I stopped and tried to tread water again, but my arms were like limp rags, slapping the water with no effect.

I tried to call out again, but it was no use.

By now the gang were busy jumping out of the boat and onto the sand without getting too wet. They weren't even looking at me.

I went under. I struggled back to the surface for just long enough to catch a breath and went under again. More struggling. More terror. And again I reached the surface.

It was all a blur. Blurry figures pulling the boat up onto the sand. Blurry figures standing still side by side looking back towards me. They seemed to be calling out, but all I could hear was a roaring in my ears.

I felt myself going down again. This time, I knew, I wouldn't have the strength to save myself. The water closed over my head.

Just when I thought it was over, I felt a hand clutching at my shirt.

9

One thing after another

'With friends like yours you don't need enemies, do you?' a rough voice said.

It was the Old Man of the Sea, looking down at me. He'd hauled me out of the water and I was lying twitching and spluttering on the bottom of his boat. Just like one of his landed fish.

'I'm not a good swimmer,' I said stupidly.

'You're not any kind of swimmer, mate,' he said. 'If I were you I'd stay well away from boats.'

'It was an accident,' I said. 'I fell out.'

'Well accidents do happen and that's a fact.'

His voice was even but you could tell he was pretty unhappy with me. I'd spoilt his fishing morning. But I could have kissed him. I kept thinking, 'This guy has just saved my life. He's the most wonderful person in the world.'

He turned up the idling motor and the boat sped in towards shore. As the bow lifted up onto the sand, the gang came running. They all looked either worried or guilty.

I climbed slowly out of the boat, still coughing. The Old Man of the Sea nodded grimly to the others and then, with the help of a push from Elmo and Sunny, headed out to sea again.

'Thank you,' I called out.

He just raised and dropped his arm without turning around. I couldn't tell if that meant 'You're welcome' or 'Get lost'. Probably both.

'Tom, we're so *sorry*!' Liz was saying, over and over again.

'Why didn't you tell us you couldn't swim?' Sunny demanded.

'He was probably embarrassed,' Richelle said. 'Well, you would be, wouldn't you?'

She looked me up and down. I felt myself blushing red. I was shivering all over. My hair was dripping and plastered to my head. My nose kept running. I knew I looked a total wreck. An embarrassing, clumsy wreck.

To add to my agony, Bliss Bell was watching us from the veranda of her house. Then the hundred-year-old couple came along carrying bread and milk and a newspaper from Skinner's. I knew they'd seen the whole drama. They shook their heads and tutted to each other as they passed.

'The very least the old bloke could have done is give

us some fish,' Nick said, trying to lighten up the situation. He had his hands in his pockets and was looking very uncomfortable. I guess he felt responsible. His little joke had backfired well and truly.

'Come on,' said Liz firmly. 'Let's get back to the house and dry off. Then we can all have something to eat.'

○

I climbed out of my wet clothes, had a hot shower and got into a dry pair of shorts and a shirt. Combed my hair and then I started to feel almost human again.

'What do you say we paint the studio and get it all over and done with?' Sunny was saying, when I came back into the living room.

'Dad said not to bother till he gets back,' I told her.

'Why wait? It's got to be done sooner or later. And it's what we're here for. It doesn't take a lot of brains to slap on a bit of paint.'

'Then we'll be perfect for the job,' called Liz from the kitchen. She was carrying out her plan of making something to eat. She obviously thought that food would cheer everyone up. Sunny, on the other hand, thought that keeping busy was the answer. Personally, I was with Liz all the way.

'Come on, you guys, we can do it. We just have to follow the directions on the tins,' Sunny insisted. 'That's all your dad would do, Tom.'

They went outside to check out the paint tins. I stayed

61

indoors next to the heater, waiting for it to warm up. Liz was cutting up cheese for toasted cheese sandwiches. I heard the griller tray on the stove rattle, and my stomach rumbled. I was ravenous. I guess nearly dying makes you hungry.

'Hey, Tom, is that thing on?' Liz called after a minute.

'What?'

'The heater.'

'No, not yet.'

'Neither's the stove,' she said. 'I think the electricity's off.'

'Oh, great. I hope Dad's got some spare fuses.'

Liz went out the front door, took a look at the fuse box, and then ran back inside.

'Hey, the wire's broken,' she exclaimed. 'It looks like it's been pulled out. Like somebody grabbed it and just pulled it.'

I got up to look. She was right. The wire that went from the fuse box into the house had been pulled loose. I opened the fuse box and took out the main fuse.

The others had come around to the front of the house to see what was happening.

'Can you fix it?' Elmo asked.

'Nup,' I said. 'Needs an electrician.'

'Who do you think did it?' Sunny asked.

'Someone who doesn't like toasted cheese sandwiches, I guess,' Liz said. 'Anyone for *un*-toasted cheese sandwiches?'

○

There were big footprints on the muddy ground near the fuse box. Could they have been made by the person who pulled the wire out? It looked like it. There were no jogger tread-marks. Just flat prints, made by an ordinary leather shoe. So the prints hadn't been made by one of us. Or by Dad.

I looked through the skinny phone book next to the telephone. There was no electrician in Banyan Bay, of course. It would have to be one of the two in Nuk Nuk. I picked up the phone. No dial tone. Nothing. The phone was dead.

Things were starting to get really weird.

I followed the telephone line from the jack on the wall, up and over a door and then through the wall to the side of the house. Surprise—the phone line had been cut too.

'Great,' Richelle said. 'I'm getting out of here. This is like one of those horror movies. First they cut the wires and then they start cutting our heads off.'

'I can't understand it,' Sunny said. 'Who would do a thing like this?'

'Come on,' I said. 'It's probably just one of the locals who doesn't like us.'

'That could be anyone. Literally,' said Nick. 'We don't seem to be too popular round here.'

'Could you fix the telephone, Nick?' Liz said. 'You're

good at that sort of stuff.'

He shook his head. 'I don't think I can do anything,' he said. 'Some of the wire's missing. There's at least a metre gone.'

'I can't believe this,' I said. 'You know what? I reckon it's that cop Bluett making trouble.'

'It's a great old-fashioned place, the Bay,' Sunny remarked.

'There's a phone box opposite Skinner's,' I said. 'I'd better go down there.'

'Let's forget it and have lunch,' Nick said. 'We can take a walk down there later. There's no rush. No-one's going to get to us today anyway.'

'You mean we're not going to have a phone, or lights or the stove or anything all *night*?' shrilled Richelle.

I nodded gloomily. What she was going to say when the hot water ran out I couldn't bear to think.

10

Getting nowhere fast

After lunching on Liz's un-toasted toasted cheese sandwiches, we all trudged off to the phone box outside Skinner's General Store.

The telephone company said they couldn't send a repairman till the next day. The first electrician said he couldn't make it till tomorrow either—tomorrow at the earliest. The second said the same. Whatever happened to competition?

I asked the second guy if there were any other electricians in the area and his answer was simple and to the point. 'Nope,' he said.

Next, after waiting ages for Directory Assistance, we all pooled our change and I rang the hospital. The receptionist there didn't know anything. She didn't even have a record of a Fay McKell, she said.

'How about Fay Moysten?' I asked, even though I knew that Fay didn't usually use Dad's name.

'Sorry, nobody here by that name either. Might they

have transferred her to another hospital?'

'I don't know, could you check?'

She went away for a minute or two.

'Sorry, dear, no luck,' her voice quacked into my ear. 'You must have been given the wrong hospital name.'

I thanked her and put the phone down, wondering what to do next.

'How about ringing your mother?' Liz said.

'I don't know,' I said. 'I'd rather not.'

Mum would only worry—if not about Fay, about us. Besides, what if Brian answered the phone? I didn't want to have to explain it all to him. I didn't even want to talk to him and I didn't want to give him an excuse to criticise Dad for leaving us alone.

Terrible thoughts started running through my head. What if Fay was dead? What if she'd really died in the car crash and they needed someone to come in and identify the body? Maybe they rang dead people's relatives and told them they were okay and would they come to the hospital. Then they could tell them the bad news in person.

No, I thought, they wouldn't do that.

Crazy thoughts. More likely Dad had told me the wrong hospital. In the state he was in, he could have done anything.

Sunny, Nick and Elmo were sitting on a rock near the bus stop talking about the cricket-ball puzzle. I said that I was going to buy some food. I told Nick it would be better if he didn't come into the shop because I was going to have to convince Mrs Skinner to put it all on Dad's account.

'I don't think she likes you,' I said.

'What a thing to say,' Nick said. 'Of course she likes me. You can tell by the way she speaks to me.'

'You get out of here, you young smart alec,' Sunny said putting on an old lady's voice.

'I'm sure she didn't mean it,' Nick said.

'I think she did.'

'Oooooh,' Nick whined, looking really hurt.

'Hey, Tom, don't forget to buy some candles for tonight,' Sunny said.

'Why?' I asked. 'So we can watch TV by candlelight?'

'Don't be stupid.'

Liz and Richelle and I went into Skinner's and collected some bread, biscuits, a packet of sliced ham, some packet sausages and a couple of tins of cooked vegies off the shelves. We also got the candles, some matches, and some firelighters so we could be sure the barbecue would light. The barbecue was our only hope of a cooked meal with the electricity off.

Then came the tough part.

'Could you put these on my dad, Mr Moysten's, account?' I asked.

'What's wrong, don't you have any money?'

'Well, actually . . . I mean the thing is . . . you see Dad's wife—I mean, Fay, my stepmother's been in an accident and Dad's had to rush to the hospital—in Sydney. And he said that you'd put anything we needed on his account.'

Mrs Skinner gave me a steely look.

'What do you need candles and firelighters for?'

'We don't have any electricity,' I explained. 'Somebody ripped the wires out. No lights, no stove. We'll have to have a barbecue.'

'If you ask me, you'd better nick off back to the city quick,' Mrs Skinner said sharply. 'By the time you're finished with that house it'll be in ruins.'

'We didn't do it,' I squeaked. 'Somebody else did.'

'Somebody else,' she muttered. 'Somebody else.'

I don't know if she believed me or not about Fay's accident. She didn't say anything. After staring at me for a minute, she rang everything up on the cash register and then wrote the cost in a book under Dad's name.

'And you shouldn't be skylarking around in the water,' she told me. (News travels fast!) 'You don't see anyone else swimming in Banyan Bay, do you?'

'Well, no,' I admitted.

'There's a good reason for it. There are sharks out there. They come in all the time. A big one came in just this morning.'

'Are you sure?'

'White pointer, it was. Came right into the bay. It's that yacht. They throw all their scraps overboard. They come in here and they ruin the place for swimmers and they don't spend a blooming cent. They—'

She broke off.

I noticed that Richelle was looking with interest at the

68

curtained doorway.

Mrs Skinner's little black eyes flashed. She leaned across and twitched the curtains more firmly closed.

'Girl about your age got taken by a shark down in Bentone last year,' she said, wagging her finger at Richelle. 'Pretty girl she was too. Sharks don't care about that.' She smiled nastily. 'Sharks couldn't care less what fool colour you paint your nails.'

❀

'What an awful woman!' hissed Richelle as soon as we got out the door. 'Have you ever heard anything so rude? Can you *believe* that?'

'Did you see someone behind that curtain?' I asked eagerly, as we walked over to join the others. I'd almost forgotten the dark figure I'd seen on our first visit to Skinner's. But now the memory came flooding back. And with it my curiosity. Full strength.

'Yes,' Richelle said. 'There was a man back there. But I couldn't see him properly.'

'I could,' Liz said. 'He's a lot younger than she is. Tall. Dark. Kind of good-looking. But your dad said she lived alone. I wonder who he is?'

'Maybe it's her son—come back to visit the old home town at last.'

'Then why's she keeping him out the back like that? Hiding him away?'

'Maybe it's not her son. Maybe she's got a boyfriend,'

Richelle giggled. 'Her toy boy.'

'You're just saying that to make me jealous,' Nick said. 'I know it's me she really likes.'

11

Splitting up

The sky had clouded over. It was still early afternoon, but now that the sun had disappeared the bay seemed cold and gloomy.

Everyone sat huddled around the living room, looking bored.

Why did I bring them here? I thought to myself. The way things are shaping up it's the stupidest thing I've ever done. Well, almost.

Sunny thought we should start painting the studio, but Liz said she was sure it was going to rain.

'We could go fishing again,' Nick suggested, with a sly look at me. He seemed to have got over his guilt pangs, anyway.

'Mrs Skinner reckons there was a white pointer in the bay this morning,' Liz told him.

'That's it!' cried Nick. 'That's what I caught. The big one that got away.'

'Your hook got caught on a rock, that's all,' Sunny said.

'Rubbish!' Nick said. He began to pace up and down the room, into the studio and out again. Then he began a slow chant that got louder and louder as it went. 'I'm bored, I'm bored, I'm bored, I'm bored, I'm bored, I'm bored, I'M BORED! BORED! BORED! BORED!'

Richelle had found a stack of magazines and had just settled down ready for a few happy hours of looking at pictures.

'Shut up, Nick,' she yawned, without looking up.

Liz glanced at her, and then frowned. She got up and went over to the paintings that were stacked against the wall behind Richelle's chair.

'Hey listen,' she said, looking through them. 'Someone's been in here. Someone besides us.'

'What do you mean?' I asked.

'Someone's been looking through these paintings. I can tell, because I neatened them all up before we went out fishing.'

'What do you mean, you neatened them up?'

'I was looking through them and I remember lining them all up—like this.' She put her left arm beside the untidy stack and pushed it till all the edges of the paintings were in a straight line.

'That's what they looked like just before we left,' she frowned. 'Has anyone here touched them since?'

We all shook our heads.

'Well, someone has.' Liz nibbled at her bottom lip.

'That's weird,' Sunny said. 'Are any missing?'

'I don't think so,' I muttered, flipping through the

boards. 'They seem to all be here.'

'Whoever cut the wires must have gone through the house, too,' said Elmo quietly.

'What'd I say? While we were fishing? I *told* you I saw somebody in here,' Richelle exclaimed. 'I *told* you I saw someone looking out the window.'

'Okay, you were right,' said Liz. 'Unless it happened when we were out at the shop just now.' Her eyes widened. 'Maybe whoever did it is still here!' she whispered.

We all looked around and I could feel my heart racing.

'Where?' Nick jeered. 'There are only two rooms. We're in here, and I've just been to the studio. There's nowhere for anyone to hide.'

'Oh, yeah?' Sunny said. 'How about the loo—and the loft?'

The thought of someone hiding in the house made me weak at the knees. Just the idea that someone had been in there prowling around was bad enough.

There were a few sticks of firewood in a basket by the fireplace. We each grabbed one. Then we tiptoed towards the bathroom. It was tiny, with only a shower, a handbasin and a toilet, and the door was partly open.

Sunny peered around behind the door. The only other place an intruder could have been hiding was behind the shower curtain.

I stepped into the room beside her. She raised her stick over her head as I threw back the curtain.

Nothing.

I gave a deep sigh. Sunny and I backed out of the

73

bathroom. I for one felt pretty silly but, before anyone spoke, Sunny put her finger to her lips and pointed up towards the loft.

Elmo climbed up first with Sunny and me right behind. The others clambered after us. Once we got to the top we could see all around. The bed was just a double-bed mattress on the floor, so there was nowhere to hide except in the wardrobe.

Sunny pulled opened the wardrobe door. Inside was a mass of clothing, mainly Fay's dresses.

Elmo poked his stick at the clothes again and again to make sure no-one was hiding behind them.

'Stop it, Elmo,' Richelle shrilled. 'You'll rip them to shreds. There's no-one in there.'

'Phew!' Nick wiped his forehead with fingers that weren't quite steady.

Liz turned to him.

'Still bored, Nick?' she asked.

'Not at the moment, thanks, Liz,' he said. 'Not at the moment.'

The more we looked around the loft, the more Liz became convinced that the house had been burgled. The drawers of Dad and Fay's chest had all been left open and everything was messed up inside them.

'It's just what burglars do,' Elmo said. 'The quickest way to search a chest of drawers is to open the bottom drawer first, run your hand around under everything as fast as you can and then open the next drawer up and so on. They don't want to push them back in because they want to get out of the house as fast as possible.'

'Dad's not exactly neat,' I said. 'It's possible he left them like this.'

'No.' Elmo shook his head. 'When you're messy you leave some drawers out and other ones in. I speak from experience.'

I nodded. He was right.

We turned our backs on the mess in the loft and climbed back down to the living room.

'How do you think the burglar got in?' Richelle asked nervously.

'Good question.' I furrowed my brow, folded my arms, and paced backwards and forwards in front of her. 'Let's see. He could have cut a hole in the roof and climbed through. But then there would have been a hole—and there isn't. He could have broken a window. He could have tunnelled through the underfloor . . . No, I've got it!'

I spun around to face her. 'Do you know what I think?' I demanded.

'No.'

'I think he turned the doorknob on the front door and walked right in. You see, there's no lock on it.'

Sunny snorted with laughter.

'Tom?' Richelle said.

'Yes?'

'Shut up.'

'Look, this is serious, guys,' Liz said. 'We'll have to ring the police.'

'We don't know if anything's missing,' I said.

'But we know somebody broke in. We should at least report that.'

'We *think* someone broke in,' I said. 'But will Sergeant Bluett agree with us?'

'Besides,' Sunny added, 'what if he's the one who broke in?'

'Yeah,' said Nick, 'maybe he ran out of oregano.'

'I still say we should report it,' said Liz stubbornly.

'I say we wait till Dad gets back, and then report it if he wants to,' I put in.

'And *I* say we catch the afternoon bus back to Nuk Nuk and then go home!' Richelle exclaimed. '*I'm* not staying in a place that gets broken into and has no lock on the door. And I don't see how any of the rest of you can think about doing it either.'

The others considered that. I watched in despair as I saw Richelle's reasoning take hold.

'She might be right,' Sunny agreed reluctantly. 'We've got no electricity or phone, remember.'

'Yeah,' said Nick. 'Of course she's right. We should get out of here.'

'I don't see why,' I objected. 'We can manage. If we're all together.'

Liz and Elmo looked at me, and then at each other.

'Actually, it is probably best we go, Tom,' Liz said gently, after a moment. 'When you think about it, Mel won't really want to be bothered with us here—with Fay in hospital and everything. We'll be more trouble than we're worth.'

I shrugged. They all trailed into the studio to pack up their things.

I shoved my sketchbook, cap and wallet into my shoulder bag. So we were leaving. Great!

The doors to the deck were open. I went over to close them, and then on impulse I went out. There was a storm brewing. It was getting darker by the minute and huge thunderheads like grey heads of cauliflower were forming just to the west.

In the houses along the beach, windows and shutters were slamming as people got ready for a storm. I could see Bliss Bell pull a roller shutter down, closing her shed.

Somewhere out there in good old-fashioned Banyan Bay was someone who had cut our wires and broken into the house.

Why? What were they up to?

Mixed-up thoughts flooded into my brain. Had the phone call about Fay's accident all been a hoax?

Had someone sent Dad on a wild goose chase?

Was the same person trying to drive us away too?

Well, if so, they weren't going to succeed. I wasn't going to give in so easily. I went back into the house and into the studio.

'Come on and pack, Tom,' urged Liz. 'We don't want to miss the bus.'

I shook my head. 'I'm not leaving,' I said.

They stared at me.

'But Tom, you can't stay here on your own!' Sunny exclaimed.

'Of course I can,' I said. 'This is my dad's house. He left me in charge. And I'm staying.'

The sky was dark with thunderclouds when we walked to the bus stop, but there was still no rain. We walked in silence. The others were feeling bad because they were running out on me. I was feeling guilty because their trip had been such a dead loss, and very embarrassed, too. What would their parents think when they came back so soon?

Sheila was waiting at the bus stop when we arrived. The driver was dozing on the front seat, but woke up when the gang climbed on board.

'Back to the big smoke so soon?' the driver asked.

'Yeah,' said Nick. 'Couldn't stand the excitement.'

'It's a great old place, the Bay,' he said. 'Got to make your own fun, of course. But there's nothing like this peace and quiet.'

He was right: we'd had nothing like peace and quiet since the moment we arrived.

'You can still change your mind, Tom,' Liz said.

'No he can't,' Nick said. 'Tom's as stubborn as you are.'

'I want to stay, really, Liz,' I said. 'I'll be okay.'

The driver glanced at his watch. 'We'll be leaving in

five minutes,' he announced. 'Rain, hail or shine.'

The sky rumbled. It looked like shine was out of the question. But rain, and even hail were certainly strong possibilities. I decided to head back to the house. I waved goodbye to the gang and started back.

❀

The road seemed to be getting longer every time I walked it.

I began thinking about all that had happened in the past twenty-four hours. The police suspicion. The real unfriendliness from Bliss Bell and Mrs Skinner. Fay's accident. The cut wires and the break-in.

What was going on in Banyan Bay? Maybe Sergeant Bluett had been right about drugs all along.

I thought about it. No-one could be growing fields full of marijuana because the police—even Bluett—would have found them by now. Besides, Banyan just isn't a place where people grow things. There are cows up on the hills, but no crops.

But maybe the fact that it was such a quiet out-of-the way place made it a perfect place for smuggling. Shipments of hard drugs could be coming in here by sea and then taken on to the cities.

Bliss Bell, I thought. Could she have anything to do with it? She had enough money to buy the houses on either side of hers just to have some privacy. She'd have to sell a lot of sculptures to get that kind of money.

Maybe sculpture was just a cover and she'd found a better way to get rich.

Or maybe Mrs Skinner's black sheep son was the villain. *If* it was him we'd seen hiding in the back of the shop. And if that was the case, did that mean Mrs Skinner was involved in the drug-smuggling too? And all that crabby old lady stuff was an act?

Dad's house was up ahead. I peered at it, jumped, then peered again. For a moment I thought I'd seen a flickering light at one of the windows.

'You're spooked, Tom,' I said aloud. 'Get a grip on yourself.'

Thunder rumbled as I reached the house. It was so dark now that you'd have thought it was evening. I pushed open the front door. It was even darker inside.

Where were those candles? Now I remembered. They were on the kitchen bench. I walked towards the kitchen with a hand out to make sure I didn't bump into something.

There was a tiny sound behind me. I remember that. But I had no time to turn around. Because the next second the world had exploded in a shower of stars and I was crashing to the floor. My head hit the boards.

And then I knew nothing at all.

12

In deep water

When I woke up there was a high wind outside and the floor was lurching violently. Suddenly I knew that I wasn't in Dad's house anymore.

Was I alive or was I dead? My head was nearly splitting. The back and forth motion started and stopped and then started again, setting my stomach churning. I felt as though I was going to be sick.

I forced my eyes open and saw small lights on the wall. They seemed to be moving up and down. Everything was moving up and down.

Suddenly I knew where I was. I was on a boat. And somehow I knew which one. I was inside the big white yacht.

I heard a door open behind me, and the sound of voices. Quickly I closed my eyes and pretended that I was still unconscious. By opening my eyelids a tiny bit I could just make out the shapes of the two men standing above me. One was tall, one was short. The short one was wearing a white jacket. He was carrying my shoulder bag.

'It was stupid, bringing him here,' the short one said.

'What else was there to do?'

'The orders were no contact with land, Fritz. No contact. What if someone saw them? What if they were followed?'

'No-one saw them. No-one followed them,' growled the big man. 'Not in this weather. And what was the boss supposed to do, Ace? Crack the kid on the head and just leave him there? With what he knows?'

'Why not?'

'Are you kidding? Half-an-hour after he woke up this town'd be crawling with cops. Then the whole plan'd be up the creek. This way we can find out what the kid knows, and then we can get rid of him.'

That didn't sound too good. My throat seemed to close up, and I choked.

'Hey, he's coming around!'

The big man called Fritz pulled me up by my arms to a sitting position. I slowly opened my eyes and looked at the two men properly. There was nothing unusual about them. One was big and the other one was small, that's all. They just looked like ordinary guys. But they weren't.

I put my hand to my head and swallowed. 'Did—did I fall down on the road?' I stammered, trying to look vague. 'Did you find me? I must have hit my head. I can't remember anything. It's all a blank. Thanks a lot for looking after me. But I'm okay to go home now, if you'll just . . .'

I tried to get to my feet, but the cabin started to spin and I sat down with a thump again.

The men were both laughing. Or at least their mouths were laughing. Their eyes looked cold as ice.

'Good try, kid,' Ace said. 'But we didn't come down in the last shower. You know what happened all right. And now you can tell us a few things. What's your name?'

'Tom.' I licked my lips. I was having trouble making them move.

'Tom what?'

'Tom Moysten,' I mumbled.

They looked at each other. 'You're telling us you're related to Mel Moysten?' said Fritz.

'He's my father.' I blinked, trying to clear my head. They knew Dad's name. What was going on here?

'What are you doing in Banyan?' Ace asked. 'You and your mates?'

'We've been staying here with my father,' I said. 'I mean, we just came for a holiday.'

'A holiday, huh?' Ace sneered. 'In this miserable hole? Listen, kid, I told you. Don't mess around with us. Or you'll be sorry. How long has your father—if he is your father—been working for the cops?'

I just stared at him. He bent over and slapped my face.

My head snapped back and a bolt of pain shot through it. My eyes started to water.

'Answer the question,' Fritz snarled.

'He doesn't work for the cops,' I muttered. 'He's a painter.'

Slap!

'You're not a very fast learner are you, Tom?'

'I'm telling you the truth!' I yelled. 'You want the truth, don't you?!'

Just then there was a thump and a shout outside. Ace cursed and went out, slamming the door behind him and leaving big Fritz to stare worriedly at me, his hands in his pockets.

There was a short silence and then more shouts and thumps and a noise like someone was falling against the wall just outside the door. Fritz half-turned to look. I started trying to get up, but he reached out and and pushed me back down without even turning his head.

The cabin door flew open and a man was pushed through. He stumbled and fell to the floor with a crash.

It was the Old Man of the Sea.

He crouched there on his hands and knees, shaking the hair out of his eyes.

Ace followed him in. And now had a gun in his hand.

'So no-one followed them?' he barked at Fritz. 'Well who's this, you clown? Now we've really got trouble. This guy's a local. Getting rid of the kid's one thing. Getting rid of this guy's something else.'

Fritz just stood there, his mouth hanging open.

'Come on!' snapped Ace. 'I'm going to have to tell the boss about this. And you're coming with me.'

He turned to me. 'I'll see you later,' he snarled.

He jerked his head at Fritz and they left the cabin. I heard the click of a bolt being thrown on the other side of

84

the door.

The man on the floor gingerly felt his jaw through his tangled beard, shook his head, and winced. I crawled over to him.

'Are you all right?' I said. Pretty stupid thing to say, I know. He wasn't all right. Neither of us was all right.

He scowled. 'That'll teach me to stick my nose in,' he said. 'I saw you getting carted off, so I came over in the boat to get a better look. My mistake was getting on board.' He shrugged. 'Curiosity killed the cat.'

'We're not dead yet,' I said, trying to smile.

He painfully moved himself into a sitting position. 'Maybe not,' he said grimly. 'But from the sound of things we soon will be.'

He closed his eyes. 'I should have just gone and rung Bluett,' he went on. 'But saving you seems to have got to be a habit with me.'

'Who are those guys?' I asked.

'Search me. Don't you know?'

'They've got some racket going on. Drugs, maybe. Something like that, anyway. They keep going on about my dad working for the police.'

He looked at me under his bushy eyebrows.

'Mel Moysten's a cop?'

'Of course not. They just think he is. They think I know something about them. And they've been searching Dad's house. Someone was there when I got back from seeing the others off on the bus. I didn't see who it was. I got hit on the head, and I woke up here. That's all I know.'

'Are you sure, son? Don't keep me in the dark.'

I held up my hand. 'I swear,' I said. 'And it's crazy to think Dad's with the police. Bluett picks on him. He can't stand him. He thinks Dad's a druggie himself!'

'Oh, Bluett.' The man's mouth twisted in a smile of contempt. 'These guys wouldn't care about him. If you're right, and this is a drug racket, they'd be talking about the Commonwealth police or the drug squad.'

Oh. I shook my head. 'I can't understand why they'd think Dad was involved. He's a painter. He used to be an architect. He moved here for the peace and quiet.'

The man grinned, showing even, white teeth. 'Like me,' he said. 'Well, looks like we both picked the wrong place, doesn't it? Especially your old man. See, that boathouse of his—well, can you think of a better place to live if you wanted to keep an eye on things in Banyan Bay? If you were an undercover cop waiting to spring a gang of drug smugglers, for example?'

I nodded. It made sense. 'I guess that's what they thought,' I said. 'But they're wrong. Dad would never work for the police. He's not the type.'

'What about his lady?'

I shook my head. 'Fay's not the type either,' I said positively. 'No way.'

'Where are they now?' he asked. 'How come you're on your own?'

I told him about the phone call. Fay's accident. Dad rushing off. My friends leaving. He listened quietly, stroking his beard. He didn't flicker when my voice started to choke up. I turned my head away and struggled to calm myself down.

'What are we going to do now?' I managed to say.

He seemed to come to a decision. He got to his feet and pounded on the door.

'Listen you goons!' he yelled. 'It's me you want, not the kid! You let him go and I'll tell you everything you want to know!'

I gasped. He turned around to me and grinned. 'Don't worry about me,' he muttered. 'I'll spin them a line. I've been in tighter places than this.'

'But these guys don't fool around.'

'Neither do I,' he said grimly.

His voice sounded so confident that I suddenly felt better. I had no idea what he was going to do, but obviously he had something up his sleeve.

'What's your surname?' I asked. It sounded stupid, after all we'd been through. But I thought I should know. I couldn't really ring Sergeant Bluett and say I'd been kidnapped, and so had Harry, the Old Man of the Sea. He'd think I was nuts.

He smiled. 'Faber. Harry Faber.'

The bolt rattled and the door opened a crack. Big Fritz's face appeared, glaring at us.

'He doesn't know anything,' Harry said, jerking his head at me. 'It's me you want. You tell your mate that if you let the kid go I'll spill the beans.'

Fritz growled and pulled the door shut again. The bolt shot home. He was being careful. No way was he going to make any mistakes.

A few long minutes passed.

'Cross your fingers,' Harry drawled.

With a clatter the door opened again. Fritz jerked his head at me and I went over to him. Then, without any warning, he pulled me roughly out of the cabin. It all happened so fast that I didn't have time to call out.

He held on to me with an iron grip as he shot the bolt, locking Harry in again. Then he started hauling me along a narrow passage and up a ladder to the deck.

It was as dark as night out there. I gasped as cold wind and spray hit me in the face. Fritz pulled me along to where Ace was standing in the stern, all done up in a shiny yellow anorak and holding the bag with my sketchbook and wallet in it.

The yacht was rolling from side to side and a wave hit the side, sending spray up and over us. The yacht's dinghy bobbed wildly around in the water. I saw that Harry's boat was tied to it.

'Well?' Fritz said. 'What do we do with him?'

'What do you think?' snarled Ace. 'Throw him overboard.'

My legs went rubbery and I collapsed on the deck.

'Stand up!' Ace ordered. He hooked my bag over my head. 'They might need this to identify you, kid,' he said. 'Few days in a sea like this mightn't leave you looking all that pretty.'

'But you made a deal!' I screamed. 'You're supposed to let me go!'

They both laughed.

'We *are* letting you go,' said Ace. 'All you have to do is dog-paddle home. The tide's strong round here. You'll be away from the yacht in no time.'

Fritz grabbed me, with one arm around my neck and the other arm under my legs. He heaved me towards the side.

'But I can't swim!' I yelled. 'I can't swim!'

'Tell us something we don't know,' Ace sneered.

'Tell you what, kid,' sniggered Fritz. 'When your feet hit the bottom, start running!'

'Please!' I begged. 'I'm not kidding! I can't swim!'

'Which is why we don't have to shoot you first,' Alf said. 'It's very handy. This way it'll look just like an unfortunate accident. Like you fell off the boathouse deck in the storm.' He nodded to Fritz. I felt the big man's muscles tense.

'There's a shark in the bay!' I yelled desperately. I couldn't believe this was happening to me.

Ace grinned. 'Is there now? That'll make it even more tragic.'

Fritz heaved, and I felt myself falling through the air and plunging, headfirst, out and down into the pitch black water.

13

Escape to danger

It was my worst nightmare come true. I struggled helplessly, spinning in black water, not knowing which way was up. I forced myself not to scream. I knew that if I did the water would rush into my mouth and down into my lungs.

Then I'd be finished.

As if I wasn't finished anyway.

My head broke the surface. The current had already swept me away from the yacht. I could see its lights moving as it tossed up and down. Near. But not near enough.

My heart beat suffocatingly as I struggled to stay afloat. Water rolled up into my face, covering my mouth and nose. Black water. Deep water.

I started thinking about my legs, kicking helplessly down there in the darkness. The white pointer. Was it nosing its way towards me right now, attracted by those pale, moving shapes? Would I feel it grab me any minute? Any second?

I yelled, though I knew no-one would hear. The wind

and the waves drowned out everything. Another wave rolled over me. I went down, kicking, struggling.

Then something grabbed my arm.

I screamed, thrashing against its dragging grip. I felt the water rush into my mouth. This is it, I thought. I'm going to die.

'Tom!'

The voice reached me through a haze of fear. Did I dream it?

'Tom! Stop fighting me, you buffoon! Stop struggling! They'll hear us!'

I opened my screwed-up eyes, trying to focus through the stinging saltwater and the darkness. I was on the surface again.

And there bobbing beside me, his black hair wet and slick as a seal's, was Nick.

❁

Around his waist was a heavy rope. He looped it around me too, and tugged. And then we were being pulled together through the water.

I didn't ask myself how it was happening. I didn't ask myself how Nick could have suddenly appeared beside me in the middle of a dark, churning sea when he was supposed to be waiting for a bus in Nuk Nuk.

It was like some sort of dream. In fact, for all I knew I *was* dreaming. For all I knew I was really sinking to the bottom of the bay, having fantasies about being saved while I drowned.

But then I saw the boat. Dad's little boat. And inside it, holding out their arms to us, Sunny, Liz and Richelle.

They dragged me on board, and pulled Nick in after me. We lay panting on the bottom of the boat, on coils of wet, prickly rope. My shoulder bag was a sodden weight against my chest.

Sunny and Liz took the oars and started pulling for shore. Richelle crouched over us.

'What . . .' I spluttered. 'What are you doing here?' I choked and coughed. Nick pushed me over onto my side. I started heaving, coughing up water.

'Never mind,' he whispered. 'Don't talk!'

'We decided we couldn't leave,' murmured Richelle. 'We didn't want to leave you alone. There were too many things wrong. We got off the bus again. And then we got back to the house just in time to see you being taken away in the dinghy. So Elmo went to ring the police, and we followed you. Then we saw them throw you overboard. And Nick went out to get you. Oh, it was so scary!'

Scary is right. With an enormous effort I lifted my head so I could see over the lurching side of the boat. There was the yacht. It wasn't very far away at all. Its lights made it look like a floating birthday cake as we drew away towards the shore. There didn't seem to be anyone on deck. Ace and Fritz were down below—with Harry.

'They've got Harry—the fishing guy—the Old Man of the Sea,' I croaked. 'We've got to save him.'

'Never mind that, we've got to save ourselves first,'

Nick said. He shivered and turned to watch Liz and Sunny battling the wind and the choppy water.

Sunny was managing, but Liz was getting very tired. You could see it.

'Liz, get into the bow,' Sunny called. 'Nick, take over!'

Nick crawled into Liz's place. He must have been exhausted too. But he grabbed Liz's oar and did his best.

I just lay there, helplessly shivering and coughing. What a disaster! Here I was again, sprawled on the bottom of another boat—terrified, half-drowned and unable to lift a finger.

I was hysterical, I guess. I started laughing, pressing my hands against my mouth to keep myself quiet though I knew the wind would mask the noise.

Richelle, thinking I was crying, rubbed my shoulder nervously. 'It's all right,' she said. 'You're safe now.'

I started laughing even harder. Safe? Did the girl know what she was saying?

The boat had been pointed directly at Dad's, but there was a strong headwind and no matter how hard Sunny and Nick pulled we just kept drifting sideways.

'We'll try for the beach, Nick,' Sunny yelled. 'It'll be quicker.'

They turned the boat and pulled, with all their strength.

A big wave came up behind and began carrying us along with it towards the beach. Sunny wrenched an oar out of the rowlock and thrust it at Richelle.

'We need a rudder,' she said. 'Quick!'

Richelle put the oar in the water behind her.

'What am I supposed to do?' she yelled.

'Just keep us going straight!' Nick shouted. 'Hold it against the back there. Point it down! Come on, Rich, work it out!'

Richelle had no idea. The oar dragged uselessly behind and, as the boat turned in front of the wave, it moved to one side.

'Not like that!' Sunny called.

Nick jumped up and was about to sit in the stern when the boat swung around ninety degrees and the wave broke over the side, swamping us.

Dad kept a plastic ice-cream container on the bottom of the boat, to use as a baler. Liz grabbed it as it floated past her and began scooping away furiously at the water. But of course it was hopeless.

The next wave caught us in the middle and sent us sprawling into the sea. This time my head was only under water for a second before it came up again.

'We'll have to swim for it,' Sunny called.

She and Nick grabbed me by the shirt and began pulling me in towards shore. The surf pushed and beat at us. Every time a wave came over us I thought we were done for, but when I came up, Nick and Sunny were still pulling.

In a few minutes the five of us lay panting on the sand.

I saw Liz get to her feet and start staggering towards the nearest house. It was Bliss Bell's. The shed door was closed but the light inside shone through the cracks between the boards at the sides.

My heart gave a huge thump. 'No, Liz!' I gasped. 'Not there!'

She hardly paused. 'Tom, we've got to get to a phone,' she said, and ploughed on over the sand. 'She won't mind. It's an emergency!'

'It's not that!' I got up and tried to go after her. But I had no strength in my legs. Coughing and spluttering, her hair wild and sticky for once, Richelle followed. Nick and Sunny took my arms and pulled me along behind.

Liz pounded on the shed door and then bent and pulled it up without waiting for an answer. Bliss Bell was standing in front of a line of wooden crates with piles of packing material on the floor next to her.

She spun around. Her face was a mask of anger.

'You!' she hissed. And lumbered towards us.

14

Bliss

'Please!' Liz cried, stumbling back with her hands up as if to protect herself. 'We need help!'

The huge woman stopped. A strange expression crossed her face. She seemed suddenly to notice the state we were in.

'What's wrong?' she asked. 'You're all wet. What's happened?'

'The police!' said Nick. 'We have to ring and tell them where we are.'

She frowned. 'What's happened?' she repeated. 'Look, come into the house.' She moved quickly out of the shed and pulled the door shut behind her.

She wouldn't listen to anything else until we were in the house. She twitched the curtains shut, and turned on the lights. And then she insisted on getting us rugs and towels. We stood there at the edge of her little kitchen-living room, dripping pools of water all over the shiny timber floor while she ratted through a cupboard.

We all just looked at each other. She turned around with her arms full.

'Come on, kids,' she said. 'Get inside. I don't care about a bit of water.'

It was warm in that little room. Deliciously warm. And so was the rug Bliss Bell wrapped me in.

'Sit down,' she said, giving me a little push. 'Before you fall down.'

I sank down in a chair. It was soft and luxurious. I was trembling all over. With a huge effort I heaved my bag off my neck and fell back, trying hard to concentrate on what was going on around me.

'We need to talk to the police,' Nick was saying. 'Elmo—our friend—was ringing them from Skinner's. They'll be there now, probably. At the shop. Could you call?'

Bliss frowned, and hesitated. Everything went still. I stared around at the others. They all looked strangely unreal in the yellow light. Things were moving too fast for me.

'Harry,' I gasped. 'Harry Faber—the fisherman. They're holding him on that yacht out in the bay. They had me too, but I got away. I think they're drug smugglers. He's in danger. We've got to get help before they kill him.'

The big woman looked at me for a long moment. Then she firmed her lips, picked up the phone, and punched in some numbers.

'Hello, Elsie,' she said, after a moment. 'This is Bliss Bell. Sorry to disturb you. Is Bluett with you, by any chance?'

Even in the trance I was in, I realised that this phone call was a major event. Imagine Bliss Bell and Elsie Skinner talking again, after years and years of ignoring one another. They weren't exactly chatting. In fact, Bliss's voice sounded very strained and formal. But they were making contact, at least.

'All right,' Bliss said, after a moment. 'Could you put him on?'

She put her hand over the phone. 'He is there,' she said. She sounded almost surprised, as though she hadn't really believed us.

She turned her attention back to the phone. 'Sergeant, it's Bliss Bell,' she said. 'There's been some trouble. I've got Mel Moysten's son and four of his friends here . . . Yes, I know, but I don't think they're joking . . . It's got something to do with that yacht in the bay.'

'Drugs,' I whispered. 'Tell him—'

She raised her heavy eyebrows. 'Mel's son seems to think they're smuggling drugs,' she said into the phone. 'Yes, he was on the yacht but he got away.'

She listened again, then glanced at me. 'He says they're still holding Harry Faber out there,' she said. 'He thinks Harry's in danger . . . Yes . . . Right . . . No, no-one else knows they're here . . . Right . . . Will do.'

She put the phone down.

'He said he wants you to sit tight till he gets here,' she told us. 'He doesn't want you to have any contact with the outside. In case . . .'

'In case what?' Richelle burst out. She was nearly in

tears. 'I can't stay here,' she wailed. 'I've got to get some dry clothes on, and wash my hair. I've just got to!'

'It's because Bluett thinks someone in Banyan Bay is co-operating with the drug smugglers, isn't it?' I said to Bliss. 'That's why he doesn't want us to be seen. He doesn't want the crims to know I didn't drown.'

She shrugged her huge shoulders. 'I don't know what he thinks or what he wants,' she said. 'All I know is what he said. We're supposed to turn off the lights and pretend there's no-one at home. And we're supposed to sit tight. Ring no-one. Answer the door to no-one. Except him.'

She switched off the main light, then reached across to a lamp standing on a side table. I blinked at it in surprise. It was in the shape of two smiling snakes in hats and sunglasses. A Dixie lamp! I wouldn't have expected an arty type like Bliss to go in for stuff like that.

'Oh, it's a Dixie lamp!' snuffled Richelle, her threatened tears turning into a wobbly smile as she shuffled over in her blanket to inspect it.

Bliss Bell shuffled her feet uncomfortably. 'Silly thing, isn't it?' she said awkwardly. I could see that she was embarrassed.

'I think it's *gorgeous*!' cooed Richelle. 'All the Dixie lamps are. They're brilliant!' She seemed to have forgotten all about being wet.

'What about that shower you wanted?' Bliss said hurriedly. 'You can use my bathroom. You all can. I'll put your clothes in the drier. And who'd like a cup of hot chocolate?'

'Me, please!' exclaimed Liz gratefully.

She wasn't alone. I decided on the spot that I'd been wrong about Bliss Bell. She wasn't nasty. She wasn't suspicious or unfriendly. She was wonderful. And so was her warm little house. It might be shabby on the outside, but inside it was really nice. Full of soft, beautifully patterned rugs, and lovely vases and very comfortable chairs.

Bliss lit a candle, and showed Richelle the bathroom. 'The rest of you can take it in turns,' she said, coming back. 'I've got a torch so I can see to make the chocolate. This is all very exciting, isn't it?' She seemed to have got quite girlish all of a sudden.

'It'll be even more exciting when storm-trooper Bluett gets here,' Nick said. 'What do you think of him, Miss Bell?'

'Oh, just call me Bliss, dear. Everyone does,' Bliss Bell said, moving around in the kitchen. 'Sergeant Bluett? Oh he's not a bad stick, is he?'

'That's guy's no stick,' Sunny said. 'He's more like a club.'

'Well he's always been nice to me,' Bliss Bell said. 'But I'm sure he can be difficult when he wants to be. He takes his job very seriously.'

'Very seriously,' I mumbled. 'He's probably strip-searching Elmo looking for aeroplane glue as we speak.'

'Who do you suppose the Banyan Bay crook is?' pondered Liz. 'It's weird. I mean, there's hardly anyone here.'

'It'd have to be someone who could take delivery of the stuff here and then get it out to the city without it seeming odd,' said Nick.

Bliss Bell smiled as she came back into the living room with steaming pottery mugs of hot chocolate. 'I don't see how anyone could do that,' she said, beginning to hand them out.

I nodded violently. 'Lots of people around here could,' I said. 'I've been thinking about it.'

'Sherlock Moysten,' jeered Nick.

I was feeling light-headed. I knew I wasn't making much sense. But I was eager to talk. Bliss waited, with her head on one side.

I took a sip of hot chocolate. The hot liquid streamed down my throat, blissfully warming me through and through.

'For instance, I thought it might be you for a while, Bliss,' I admitted recklessly. 'You could hide the heroin or cocaine, or whatever it is, in your sculptures, and send it out of town that way couldn't you?'

Nick jumped slightly and frowned at me. But Bliss didn't seem upset. She just went on looking at me, sipping her chocolate, as I plunged on.

'And, like, you're so keen on privacy,' I burbled. 'You get so angry when people like us come near you. Even outside, in the shed before, you didn't want us to see what you were packing. Did you? But why? What's the deep, dark secret?'

There was a sudden, awkward little silence.

101

Richelle came strolling into the room, holding her candle and wrapped from head to foot in a vast sarong. 'That's so much better!' she sang blithely. 'And what a *gorgeous* bathroom! Who's next?'

She stared around the room. 'What's up?' she asked.

There was a sharp knock on the back door. Everyone jumped.

Bliss strode to the door, frowning furiously.

'Bluett,' came the low voice.

Bliss unlocked the door and pulled it open. Sergeant Bluett strode in, with Elmo right behind him. They both stood there in the darkness. The policeman shone his torch around the room to see who was there. When it landed on me I could see Elmo's eyes light up.

'Tom!' he grinned. 'You're okay!'

He ran over to me and clapped me on the back.

'Okay, you kids, settle down,' Bluett rumbled. He turned the key in the back door and put it in his pocket. 'Now, I won't have any mucking around,' he ordered. 'Everybody stays put till I say you can leave.'

He glanced at Bliss Bell and strode to the front door. There was no key to lock that from the inside, so he dragged a chair in front of it and sat down.

'You may as well all take a seat,' he said, switching off his torch and stretching his legs out in front of him. 'It's going to be a long, long wait.'

15

House arrest

'Don't you want to know what happened?' I asked him.

'There'll be plenty of time for that later, sonny.'

'No, that's Sunny over there,' I said, pointing, 'I'm Tom.'

'Don't get smart with me.'

'You don't care that there's a guy out there on that yacht who's being held captive by drug smugglers?' I asked.

'Yeah, I know. Harry Faber.'

'It doesn't bother you that they might kill him?' I asked.

'Nothing to do with me,' Bluett said. 'Or with you. We're going to stay right here and wait further orders.'

'Orders from who?'

'From higher up. Now you just sit still and stop causing trouble.'

'Listen, Sergeant, I'm going to Sydney at first light,' said Bliss Bell. 'I've got some work to deliver.'

'Sorry, Miss Bell. You're not going anywhere,'

rumbled Bluett.

She drew herself up. Her eyes flashed in the gloom.

'Oh, yes I am!' she exclaimed.

'Oh, no you're not,' he muttered.

Her whole body seemed to swell with rage. She strode to the phone and picked up the receiver. Her jaw dropped.

'It's dead!' she exclaimed.

Bluett shrugged and half-smiled. 'I wonder how that could have happened,' he said.

I jumped up. My head swam a bit, but I managed to stay upright.

'Where do you think you're going?' the policeman asked.

'I don't think—I know,' I said. 'I'm going back to Dad's boathouse.'

'Sit down.'

'You can't keep us here.'

'Sit down!'

'Tom . . .' Liz began. But I took no notice. I walked to the front door. Bluett stood up so he blocked the doorway.

'Will you please get out of the way so I can go out?' I asked.

'Are you deaf, boy? Sit down!'

'Are you charging us with a crime?' Elmo asked quietly, from his chair. He was very pale. 'You can't hold us without charging us.'

'If I have to charge you, I will!' snarled Bluett. 'In the meantime you're assisting me with my enquiries and you're not allowed to leave.'

'Okay,' Nick said. 'Enquire.'

'What?'

'If we're assisting you with your enquiries, then start enquiring. What are the questions? We're perfectly willing to co-operate. If you don't have any questions, then let us leave.'

Sergeant Bluett drew his gun and looked at it thoughtfully.

'You're going to co-operate by being quiet and staying put,' he said calmly. 'And this is one good reason.'

'This is outrageous,' hissed Bliss Bell.

'Now you're going to shoot me, is that it?' I said.

'Tom,' Sunny said. 'Stop.'

Bluett leaned back

'You heard her, Tom,' he said.

My knees were trembling. I was as weak as a kitten after the knock on the head and my time in the water.

I turned and walked back to my chair. There just wasn't anything else I could do.

It was a weird evening. We went one by one to have a shower. Bliss dried our clothes. I propped my sketchbook and other stuff in front of the heater to dry. We ate baked beans and bacon on toast. Sergeant Bluett sat like an ugly statue against the front door, watching everything that went on.

Every now and then he'd tweak the front window

curtain aside to look out. From where I was sitting I got a good view when he did.

The storm had broken now and the sky was clearing. The moon played on the choppy water of the bay, so thousands of little pinpoints of light shone on the black surface like broken glass.

As the night went on, nothing happened. Bluett let Bliss go off to her bedroom, but the rest of us had to stay in the room with him.

One by one the others all went off to sleep.

Richelle lay down on one end of the lounge with her legs curled up. Liz spread herself out across two chairs. The rest of us were either on chairs or, in Sunny's case, lying on the floor on a pile of cushions.

Bluett didn't seem to sleep at all. Every time I looked towards the front door I saw his eyes, watching me through the darkness. It seemed to me that I was awake all night, too, but I must have slept, because suddenly it was light outside.

Bluett was sitting in his chair, still wide awake. He'd moved to one side of the door and pulled the curtains aside so he could look out at the beach and the sea beyond.

At first I thought that the others were all still sound asleep, but then I realised that Sunny was watching the big policeman through half-closed lids, studying him closely.

Was she about to make a run for it?

I stood up quietly and looked out through the gap in the curtains. Everything was peaceful and calm. The yacht still bobbed up and down at anchor way out in the bay. There was no sign of Dad's boat. Either it had sunk to the bottom or someone had removed it in the night.

The water was glittering in the early morning light. The beach was smoothed clean after the storm. A few seagulls waddled around. The hundred-year-old couple strolled along arm in arm towards Skinner's shop. Safe, calm, peaceful Banyan Bay.

Bluett made a small sound, and leaned forward. He'd seen something. Suddenly I saw a small boat coming towards the beach. I squinted against the glare, and recognised the red-and-blue markings. It was Harry!

Bluett spoke to me without turning around.

'Hey you,' he said. 'Sit back down.'

Did the guy have eyes in the back of his head?

'I'm just looking,' I said.

'I said, sit down!'

The loud voice woke everyone up. One by one people started crawling to their feet. Bliss appeared from the bedroom wearing a vast purple caftan, her black hair a tangled shawl around her shoulders. But Bluett had apparently decided to ignore us, because he didn't say any more. He just went on staring out the window, very intently now.

He was watching Harry's boat cruising into shore. And there was Harry himself, jumping out.

He looked tired, and his hair and beard were wild, but

he heaved the boat up on the beach in the normal way and started pulling out his fishing gear just as he always did. He was safe!

Or was he? My happy exclamation stuck in my throat. Something wasn't right here. I could feel it.

Bluett pulled the curtain further away from the window and peered down the beach. I quietly moved around to see what he was looking at.

The hundred-year-old couple were still toddling along towards the shop. But coming fast in the opposite direction was someone else.

A tall thin guy in a black tracksuit was jogging along the beach towards the boat. As he moved closer I felt Liz grip my arm. 'It's the bloke from the back of Mrs Skinner's shop,' she whispered.

'That's Andy Skinner!' Bliss growled, looking over our shoulders. 'I'd recognise that face anywhere.'

Suddenly her eyes narrowed. 'He was there last night, when I was talking to you and Elsie, wasn't he?' she hissed at Bluett. 'I thought she sounded strange.'

She watched him, with her head on one side. Then stepped forward. 'What's going on here? Just which side are you on, Sergeant Bluett?'

'Keep back,' Bluett ordered harshly.

My heart was in my mouth. I felt paralysed as I watched the thin black figure slow down and come to a stop at Harry's side.

They started talking.

'I've been in tight places before,' Harry had told me.

He was tough. He could handle himself. But how could he protect himself if he didn't suspect danger? He'd escaped from the yacht. He'd reached the beach. He thought he was home and safe. But he'd fallen straight into a trap.

Suddenly I couldn't stand it any more. Harry had saved my life. I couldn't just stand there and watch this happen. I had to warn him. I had to tell him what was happening while he was still out in the open where everyone could see.

This could be my last chance!

I darted for the front door. Bluett spun around, grabbing my shirt.

'Get back!' he snarled.

I twisted violently to one side and broke his grip. I had the door open in a flash. I heard Sunny yell and Liz and Nick shout, 'Run for it, Tom! Run! Run!' as I hurled myself away from the house, over the dunes and down onto the beach.

'Harry!' I screamed. 'Look out! It's a trap! Run, Harry run!'

I saw Skinner turn sharply, his face twisted with rage.

I saw the hundred-year-old couple turn and stare.

And then Harry had shoved Skinner in the chest, knocking him to the sand. And he was off, still holding his fishing basket, pounding away along the beach.

'Run!' I bellowed. If Harry could get to the bush behind Skinner's store he could get away.

I heard the sound of Bluett, roaring as he stumbled

down from the house towards me. And then I remembered the gun.

'Run!' I screamed again.

Skinner was on his feet now. And racing after Harry. He was fast. Very fast.

But I'd given Harry a good start. He was nearly at the spot where the old couple were standing now. After that it was only a minute or two to the shop, and the bush beyond. He was going to make it!

And then I got the shock of my life. The old people were moving. Faster than I would have thought possible. The man was hurling himself forward and, with a flying tackle, bringing Harry to the ground. And then the woman was leaping on Harry as well, twisting his arm behind his back.

I watched, gaping, as they hauled him to his feet and pulled him, stumbling towards Skinner.

I turned to run, but I was too slow. Bluett had me in a grip of iron.

'Let me go!' I screamed. But he was pushing and dragging me to where Skinner was standing, yelling into a mobile phone.

'Go in now!' he was shouting. 'Now, now! Quick, before they dump the stuff. We've got problems here!'

A police launch came tearing around the breakwater and began making for the yacht.

My jaw dropped. All the fight went out of me. The whole world seemed to have turned upside down. I looked wildly at Skinner, at the hundred-year-old couple man-handling Harry Faber to the ground, at Harry's fishing basket, that Skinner was pulling open and up-ending.

Six plump fish fell onto the sand.

Skinner pulled out a pocketknife and ripped the belly of one of them open. Out fell three packets of white powder. He pulled one of the bags open, smelled it and then put a tiny bit on his tongue with his finger.

'Cocaine,' he said.

He bent over the man lying on the beach.

'I thought your fishing luck was just a bit too good, Harry,' he said grimly. 'We'd all do better if we had a skindiver to hook our fish on for us, wouldn't we?'

Then his voice changed. 'Harold Leslie Dawkins alias Harry Smithers, alias Harry Faber,' he droned. 'I am placing you under arrest. You will be charged with trafficking in a prohibited substance,' he droned. 'You have the right to remain silent . . .'

It was all over.

16

An end to the mystery

'That was a close call, Tom,' Andy Skinner said. 'You almost gave the game away.'

The police had the men from the yacht in their launch now and were heading for the pier at the other end of the beach. Harry had been taken away. Police in plain clothes were walking in and out of his house. Along the roadway there was a line of police cars and about a dozen more cops, standing in a group. A helicopter hovered overhead.

The hundred-year-old couple had taken off their wigs and wiped off some of their make-up on their handkerchiefs. Needless to say, they didn't look a hundred years old any more. Their names were Mim Menelaus and Allen Franks. And they were cops too.

It had been a big operation. And I hadn't understood any of it. I looked around at the rest of the gang. We shook our heads at each other. Boy, had we been barking up the wrong tree.

'I had no idea,' I stammered. 'I thought Harry was a good guy.'

'Oh, he's good all right,' Andy laughed. 'He's one of the best. We've been chasing him all over the country.'

'I'm really sorry,' I said miserably.

'Well if it's any comfort to you, we never would have cracked this one without you.'

'Without me? What did I do to help?'

'You did some sketches and I'm afraid I took an unauthorised look at them in your dad's house when you kids were out fishing.'

'So it was *you* at the window,' Richelle said triumphantly. 'I *knew* I saw someone.'

'What about the sketches?' I asked.

One of the other policemen waved Andy Skinner over.

'You kids go back to Bliss Bell's,' Andy said. 'I'll be over as soon as I can get away.'

'What I can't understand,' I said, slumped in one of Bliss's chairs and munching on some toast she'd made, 'is that that Harry guy saved me from drowning, but *then* he hit me on the head. And he was going to let his mates on the yacht throw me in the bay. Why did he save me the first time?'

'He had to,' Liz said.

'What do you mean, *had* to?'

'We were all on the beach, watching. It would have been really suspicious if he didn't rescue you,' Liz said. 'Then later, out on the yacht, he pretended to have been captured while he was coming to save you again. I suppose he thought you'd spill the beans to him about whether or not your dad was a cop.'

'Is he?' Bliss asked curiously.

'No, he isn't,' a voice said. 'He didn't know anything about the operation.'

We turned around. Andy Skinner was standing in the doorway.

'Would you do us a big favour?' Elmo asked. 'Will you explain what's been going on here?'

'Sure. We owe you that much,' Andy said. 'I work for the Drug Enforcement Co-ordination Unit in Canberra. We got a tip-off that there was a big load of cocaine coming ashore in Banyan Bay. We were pretty sure that someone living here, pretending to be an ordinary local, was going to take delivery of the stuff and get it to Sydney.'

'Someone like Harry,' said Bliss. 'He's only been here a couple of months.'

'Yes. Or someone like Mel Moysten—another new arrival. But it didn't have to be a blow-in, Miss Bell,' Andy said. 'It could have been someone who'd been here quite a while. Someone who liked to keep very private, and who seemed to have more money than you'd expect.' He looked around at the comfortable living room and raised his eyebrows.

Bliss frowned. Sunny smothered a giggle.

'The Unit set up Mim and Allen to live here as an old retired couple a month or two ago. They kept an eye on things. They let us know when the yacht turned up, for example,' Andy went on. 'But they needed help. And that's where I came in.'

He stretched. 'I knew the place because I grew up here, and besides, I was a bit of a tearaway as a kid, so if any of the locals noticed me hanging around they'd never dream I was a cop. I knew I could count on Miss Bell to tell them all about me.'

Bliss cleared her throat uncomfortably. Andy grinned.

'I got myself installed at my mum's, and tried to keep a low profile while I tracked down the local who was in with the gang,' he said. 'I became pretty certain that Mel and Fay Moysten weren't involved, and started concentrating on Miss Bell here.' He grinned again. 'It was just like the old days, creeping round her house. I felt like a kid again.'

Bliss sniffed. 'Lucky I didn't see you and get Bluett on to you again,' she said gruffly.

'I'll say,' said Andy. 'Bluett didn't know a thing about this. And we didn't want him to know. After all, he could have been in on the smuggling himself.'

'The man mightn't be a crook, but he's an idiot,' grumbled Bliss. 'If he'd told us what was happening last night we wouldn't have tried to get away from him.'

'He'd been told practically nothing himself,' Andy told her. 'He had his orders—keep you out of sight—and he was sticking to them. But I'm afraid he's a bit—heavy-handed—at times.' He sighed. 'Poor old Bluett.'

'He doesn't like us,' said Sunny shrewdly. 'I guess he thought we should just shut up and do what we were told. After all, he never wanted us in Banyan Bay to start with.'

'Neither did I!' exclaimed Andy. 'When you turned up I couldn't believe our bad luck. Six teenagers poking round! I thought you'd muddy the waters. Maybe even scare off the drug-runners, just when we were so close to springing a trap.'

He laughed. 'I did everything I could to get rid of you. Sent Mel rushing off to Sydney, cut off the electricity and the phone. But you just wouldn't go!'

'What were you saying before—about my sketches?' I asked. I'd been dying to know.

'Get your book and I'll show you,' he grinned.

I went and got the sketchbook from the front of Bliss's heater. It was still damp, but not too bad. I handed it to Andy and he turned the pages carefully till he got to the 'opposites' drawing of Harry the fisherman shaved and wearing a suit.

'When I searched the house, I was looking for any clues I could pick up about you kids and your dad and stepmother. What I didn't expect to find was a picture of Harry Dawkins. You see, that's just what Harry looked like when we were watching him in Adelaide two years ago.'

'I was just making people the opposite of what they were,' I said.

'And that's just what Harry did. He grew a beard and looked grubby—just the opposite of the way he usually is. I didn't recognise him—till I saw your sketch.'

'No wonder he thought you knew something, Tom. No wonder they nabbed you and the sketchbook and tried to make you talk,' cried Liz.

'Yes,' nodded Andy. 'The picture of Harry was bad enough as far as they were concerned. But there was more. Look at this.'

He turned to my picture of Harry fishing. 'You're a very good artist, Tom. You've got a great eye for detail.'

'What do you mean?'

'Look at the bubbles in the water. There are too many of them. Lots too many. As soon as I saw them I thought: "That's it! There's a scuba diver down there! A scuba diver from the yacht. Hooking doctored fish on Harry's line. That's how they're getting the cocaine on shore." And I was right. We finally cracked the case. Thanks to you.'

Liz and Sunny patted me on the back. I felt myself blushing.

Andy spread out his hands. 'It was just a shame that Harry saw the drawings too, while he was searching the boathouse,' he said. 'That's when your troubles started. He thought you really knew something. He risked taking you to the yacht because it was dark and stormy, and he thought he'd get away with it without being seen. He nearly did, too. I never saw a thing. If your friends here hadn't acted so fast you'd be shark bait now.'

I shuddered. Suddenly city noise, smells, pollution and crime looked good to me. This peaceful life was heavy.

○

After Andy had gone, Bliss made more toast. 'To celebrate,' she said. 'Though I don't know why I'm pleased. I should be insulted. Imagine Andy Skinner thinking I was the Banyan Bay drug-runner!'

'You were the most likely person, really,' Richelle pointed out, with her usual huge tact.

'Is that so?' Bliss exclaimed, frowning.

Nick covered his face with his hands. But Richelle wasn't the least embarrassed.

'Tom says arty people don't make that much money,' she explained calmly. 'But you've got lovely things like that Dixie lamp, and these real Persian rugs—and three houses, and everything. You must have got the money from somewhere.'

Bliss slowly turned around to face her. Then, without any warning at all, she started to laugh. Her whole body shook. Tears began streaming down her cheeks.

I gaped at her. Was she crazy?

'Want to see my deep, dark secret?' she gasped. 'All right then. Follow me!'

She swept out of the door and across to the shed. She threw open the shutter door. The packing cases stood there in lines. She pulled out a bundle from one of them, and unwrapped it.

'Voila!' she hooted.

In her hand was a Dixie lamp base. A dancing

elephant in a pink tutu.

Richelle squealed. The rest of us gasped. Bliss laughed and unwrapped more bundles. A zebra in tennis gear, a gorilla in a nightcap, a flamingo in shiny black gum-boots . . . Richelle was in raptures.

'But where did you get all these?' she shouted.

'I'm Dixie,' said Bliss Bell simply.

Richelle stared at her wildly. 'But—you can't be. Dixie lives in a rainforest in the far north. I've read all about her.'

'You've read what I told my distributors to say,' giggled Bliss Bell.

'But why—why the secret?'

'If people knew Dixie was me, they'd never take my proper sculpture seriously again. I'm supposed to be an artist. I'm not supposed to make stuff like this. But, let's face it, I've got to live. Where do you think my income comes from? Not from my serious work, I can tell you. That wouldn't even pay my yearly grocery bill.'

She put her finger to her lips. 'So that's the deep, dark secret,' she said. 'And not a word. Okay?'

'Okay.'

Bliss held out the elephant in the tutu to Richelle. 'Have this, with my compliments,' she said. 'You'll just have to get it wired up, and get a simple shade. That part doesn't cost much.'

I thought Richelle was going to faint.

'Oh, thank you,' she breathed.

'You're welcome,' smiled Bliss. 'I'm always glad to meet a fan.'

❁

Dad came home that night. He'd found Fay perfectly well and happy, setting up her exhibition. As you can imagine, he was quite surprised to find out what had been going on while he was away.

We had a great week, after that. The electricity and the phone were fixed up. We walked on the beach, and lit fires and toasted marshmallows—all that stuff. We even painted the studio.

But we didn't swim. And we didn't go fishing. We'd all had enough of the water to last us quite a while. And none of us really felt like eating fish.

In quiet times I sketched, Elmo read, Sunny jogged, Nick played chess with Dad and Liz worked on her Banyan Bay collage.

It was looking good. It now had a drawing of a great white shark (done by me, of course), a couple of fish hooks and some line, a picture of a Dixie lamp, and a small plastic bag filled with sugar on it, along with shells and sand, sticks and pebbles and other stuff she'd found during the week.

She'd added a kid's party mask she'd found at Skinner's store. As a symbol, she said, of the way none of the people in Banyan Bay were quite as they seemed.

She also stuck on some oregano. Sergeant Bluett had never returned ours (too embarrassed, I guess), but Mrs Skinner got some in. Plus a few other 'fancy' things. Nick told Dad that if her shop improved, it was all thanks to him.

As for Richelle, she couldn't keep her hands off her Dixie lamp. Nick kept teasing her about it and saying that she'd be sick of it before the week was out.

'Well then I'll sell it,' she said. 'I should be able to get at least five hundred dollars for it.'

That shut him up.

❁

On our last night Nick remembered his cricket ball puzzle, and told it again. And this time, finally, Richelle heard it.

'I give up,' yawned Liz. 'Tell us the answer.'

'I don't know the answer,' Nick said.

Everyone groaned.

'What's wrong with that?' he grinned. 'I want to know the answer too. That's why I was asking you.'

Richelle blinked at him. 'But it's all perfectly logical,' she said.

'Tell us all about it, Rich,' jeered Nick.

'You're asking the wrong question about that ten cents. It's just confusing the issue,' Richelle said. 'Listen. Each of the guys pays ninety cents.'

'No, they pay a dollar and get ten cents back,' Nick said.

'Yeah, that's the same thing. They each pay ninety cents. Three times ninety is two dollars seventy, right?'

'Right.'

'Their friend takes twenty cents of that. So take away twenty cents and you have two dollars fifty, right?'

'Right again.'

'And the guy with the cricket ball gets the two dollars fifty. What's so complicated about that?'

Suddenly it all seemed so simple. So obvious. We all looked at each other and then at Richelle.

'How do you *do* it, Richelle?' I said.

'It's just a matter of seeing things straight,' she shrugged. 'And not letting lots of other stuff clutter your mind. If you do that, you just get confused.' She turned to go on lovingly wrapping her Dixie lamp, ready for the trip home.

'It's the sea air,' Sunny said, taking a deep breath. 'I think it's been good for all of us. It clears the brain.'

'Come to good old-fashioned Banyan Bay for a bit of peace and quiet,' drawled Nick. 'Clear your brain, solve unsolvable cricket ball puzzles . . .'

'And other mysteries,' grinned Liz, looking at her collage.

Dad looked at us all, and shook his head.

'Do you think you kids will ever learn to keep out of trouble?' he enquired.

'I hope not,' I said. And for once, I wasn't joking.